DESPERATE
WOMEN

Need to Talk to You

DESPERATE WOMEN

Need to Talk to You

Joan Frank

Conari Press

Portions of this book have appeared in the following publications:
Ms., Utne Reader, Los Angeles Times, Newsday, Chicago Tribune,
San Francisco Chronicle, San Francisco Examiner, Cleveland Plain Dealer,
Detroit Free Press, Sacramento Bee, Bostonia, Seattle Times,
Seattle Weekly, The New Censorship, and *Sun Dog.*

Conari Press books are distributed by Publishers Group West.

Excerpt from "The Jewish Hunter," copyright ©1989 by Lorrie Moore.
First published in *The New Yorker.*
Reprinted by permission of the Melanie Jackson Agency.

"Late Fragment" from *A New Path to the Waterfall* by Raymond Carver.
Copyright ©1989 by the Estate of Raymond Carver.
Reprinted by permission of Grove/Atlantic, Inc.

Printed in the United States of America.

Cover: Sharon Smith Design
Author photo: Cynthia Spoor
Cover photo from *True Story,* July 1937. Reprinted by
permission of The Sterling-MacFadden Partnership.

ISBN: 0-943233-68-2

Library of Congress Cataloging-in-Publication Data

Frank, Joan, 1949-
Desperate women need to talk to you / Joan Frank.
p.   cm.
ISBN 0-943233-68-2   (trade paper): $9.95
1. Middle age–United States–Psychological aspects.
2. Middle aged women–United States–Psychology.   I. Title.
HQ1059.5.U5F73   1994   94-7214
305.4–dc20   CIP

For
Deborah Gardiner
brave witness, beloved friend

If she had spurned gifts from fate
or God or some earnest substitute,
she would never feel it in that way.
She felt like someone of whom she was fond,
an old and future friend of herself,
still unspent and up ahead somewhere,
like a light that moves.

—Lorrie Moore

Acknowledgments

I wish to thank the following people for their faith and help:

My sister Andrea Carabetta, and her family.
Jack Pelletier, lifelong friend.
Superb friend and editor Mary Jane Ryan.

Henry S. Dakin,
whose extraordinary curiosity and kindness allowed me to begin,
office colleague Patrice Winchester, who supported every step,
and the Dakin family.

Editor Marla Kahn Krause of the *Chicago Tribune*,
who has warmly and unequivocally said Yes and Yes and Yes.

Editors Robin Morgan and Marcia Ann Gillespie of *Ms.*,
Peg Finucane of *Newsday*, Bret Israel of the *Los Angeles Times Magazine*,
Lynnette Lamb of the *Utne Reader*, Clint O'Connor of the *Plain Dealer*.
Bay Area editors Lyle York, Regan McMahon, and Ken Conner
of the *San Francisco Chronicle*; Mike Gray, David Talbot,
and Gary Kamiya of the *San Francisco Examiner*.

Special thanks to:
San Francisco Review of Books publisher and editor Donald Paul;
writer Victoria Nelson; attorney, mover, and shaker Lizbeth Hasse;
KPFA's resident angel Susan Stone; writer and kind friend Adair Lara.

The SWAT team: Steven Barclay, Lynn Cordell, Tom Jenkins, David Kezur,
Sarah Pollock, and Edie Powell, for long-term, unconditional care.
My fiercely good and wise best friend, the redoubtable Cindy Spoor.
My dearest advocate and soul brother, writer Tom Stevens.
The Hawaii women: Stephanie Austin, Bennie D'Enbeau,
Cynthia Conrad, and Kathy Platt, and all our intersecting circles.

Finally, especially,
loving thanks to Bob Duxbury,
for what is amounting to Severe Clear, now, and on beyond.

Contents

*To tell the truth is to give birth to yourself in the world.
Again and again and again, when you give birth to yourself,
you have seized the root powers of your life.*

— June Jordan

ESPERATE WOMEN NEED TO TALK TO YOU was originally a headline advertising telephone sex that I spotted in the live-nude-girls section of the local newspaper.

The irony was irresistible. Here was female *desperation* peddled as a siren song of throbbing desire; *need to talk*, the euphemism for ripe, raving lust. I marveled: Someone had actually sat down and composed this line, chosen these words to coax people to blurt their credit card numbers—and their *own* highly particularized needs—into the phone.

How thin the conceptual membrane, I thought, between the images: the succulent, flaring-nostril desperation boasted by the ad—and the desperation modern culture scorns and fears worse than Superman did kryptonite: women trying to make sense of midlife.

Despite all apparent progress, women broaching a certain age in the late twentieth century have had damn little to go by. Our mothers staked out what they could, somewhere on a

1

continuum between Rosie the Riveter and June Cleaver. Some of them didn't make it, lost to alcohol, depression, untimely death. And while patriarchy still has a chokehold, we who've survived to witness (and assist) its loosening grip, can report something monumental being forged.

A wise friend reminded me that the word *desperate* derives from despair, which at first confounded me: *Despair* smacks of final defeat, a dead-end cesspool—while the notion of *desperation* at least bristles with frenzied energy, with unpredictable, explosive motion. I'd now argue there's a Phoenix-from-the-ashes quality about transcending despair through an act of desperation—which is what I believe women do all the time.

I am drawn to the vitality and integrity of desperation, the in-your-face of emergency: what is left, as one writer put it, when we've no time to be elegant. Women at the mid-way point have less time, and less patience for wasting it. We now turn a refined keenness of attention to inventing lives that have shape, beauty, meaning—with or without mates and families—finding ways to feed what Germaine Greer has called hunger of the soul. The pieces that follow mean to think aloud about some aspect, or moment, of that process. All, I hope, talk desperate talk; in some manner seize your lapels and swear: *I have nothing to lose. Here is what it's really like.*

There is no escaping the youth-obsession that drives our culture, nor the still very vigorous double standard which allows men's authority and vitality to accrue with age, while subtly indicting women for growing older, as if passage of time were a character flaw. Further, the difference between rattling off such information (like memorized answers to a pop quiz) and actually experiencing it, is stunning. Automatic entrée is no longer necessarily assumed. *When it happens to you, it is news.* It is a moment in which we teeter between choices, and crave a map—any map.

I began writing these reflections as I turned forty. Many have elicited letters of cheering thanks from women in their twenties through their eighties—messages still floating back in the bottles I sent out. Hearing their stories, I discover again and again that women are miraculous. They offer unvarnished truths; each truth, a fission that sets something larger in motion, widening the limits of the known, advancing the narrative. With nothing to lose but coy artifice, they serve as our era's Cassandra, or as the boy calling the emperor naked. By cutting the crap, they save us all a lot of delusion, a lot of false leads. Clearer, saner, possibly even wiser, we get on with it. Against preposterous odds, desperate women tell all. Listen.

Eat It and Weep

I'T'S THE saddest thing on Earth for a woman to admit she can't eat anymore.

The end of my youth has served formal notice. It's the mother of all turning points. Big-time loss. Big-time transition. I mourn.

Forget high culture. Forget *nouvelle*, forget five-star. I mean simple, regular eating. What is purer, more primal, more sensuous, more unilaterally endorsed? We eat, therefore we live.

So it is tragic to arrive at the moment of adulthood when I need only look in the direction of delicious food for it to leap into my mouth and lodge in great lumps at strategic places under my skin. There it bulges buoyantly, while I claw through the closet, breathing hard, for the Liz Claiborne tent dress that looks like a choirboy's cassock. It will cover, for a day anyhow, the awful truth: that I ate too much salty Chinese food for dinner, and awoke this morning the Stay-Puft Marshmallow Man, an inflated clown, a swimming pool float, my belly and rear and thighs tumescent, the flesh puffed up around my eyes like a Shar-Pei puppy's.

My jeans must be yanked on, and my face feels as if someone's taken a bicycle pump to it. I work out like an Olympian, and what faces me in the mirror is a very tired Amazon. It's no secret—but when it happens to you, it is news. After a certain point, you wear what you eat.

Once, this wasn't so. Once, the chemistry of eating was hot and clean. Bodies metabolized whatever we put in, fast. We could pack it away—and it was wholesome, charming, a signal of health and vigor; the world smiled warmly on us while we ate with abandon. I looked and felt terrific. It was safe, it was fun, it was friendly. Like war bonds, and milkmen, and dogs named Spot.

Return with me now to the early years: two adorable little girls stuffing grapes in their cheeks until they were grossly distended, trying to make each other laugh. In those dreamy postwar days you finished what was on your plate to "earn" dessert. Then Sis and I became gourmet chefs stirring melted ice cream soup, requiring many tastings. A thousand Oreos were dunked in milk until they crumbled into the cup; we slurped up the mess happily. Burgers, malts, and candy were definitive food groups. Our eyes shone; our skin was smooth and clear. I remember one afternoon in a Santa Monica hotel room, parents away: We fed the pigeons a bit, then proceeded to eat nearly an entire loaf of white bread ourselves, spread with mayonnaise, every last damn slice. A splendid time.

College meant big bowls of granola, huge fudge sundaes, gigantic greaseburgers, ghastly quantities of liquor and drugs. We put it in our mouths first, and asked what it was later. Next morning we sprang forth shiny as new pennies. Burrito for breakfast? Hey, thanks, man.

On to cocktail-waitressing days, when I swam all afternoon, rode my 10-speed bike across town to the bar, slung the suds 'til

3 A.M., toasted my colleagues goodnight with a Black Russian, and pedaled home under the early morning stars, stopping for a bag of doughnuts and quart of milk at the 7-Eleven. I was *en forme*.

Today, to fit that *forme* into its clothes and sprint it upstairs without sobbing for breath, I may enjoy one modest meal per day. The rest of the time I must sublimate, sloshing down herb teas and chomping sugarless gum. When I slip, and start building mountains on my salad bar tray that makes checkout clerks' eyebrows waggle, I know it is time to chant the mantra that drowns out radio station K-E-A-T: Resist, Sublimate, and failing all else, Build in Antidotes. These code words address each phase of the compulsion. If one is plucky, one makes it through with maybe a few extra pieces of fruit in one's belly, instead of a quart of Haagen-Dazs.

I assure you this: When you see one of those exquisitely thin sylphs onscreen or in magazines, draped artfully against the ship's railing or the Harley or the silk sheets, a delicate glass of something pale in her slender little hand—don't kid yourself. That babe longs to grind an entire pizza, and wash it back with a few malt liquors or a tall chocolate shake. How she sublimates may not be pretty.

That said, one turns heavily back to the task, a sad Sisyphus slogging uphill, never done with it. Pushing the boulder of Moderation, steeling herself against beckoning sights and smells— and oxymoronic television images: the nymphette in denim short-shorts hopping weightless as a butterfly out of the he-man's pickup truck, taking a faked hearty bite of the big fat burrito.

There: I said the F-word. For the last time, too—I swear it.

The Evening News

S O MUCH of the time, I wind up wanting to call my father. I feel like I could dial some deliberate series of numbers on a spongy rotary telephone in the fog—the kind you dream, whose dial never quite lets you poke the right hole or pull it back to the finger-stop as far it should go; a murky, squishy machine; agony of effort—yet somehow, in my dream, I'd succeed and after a moment, hear my father's mellifluous query at the other end: *Hello—o?*—that lilting second syllable urging us all to be well, to be reasonable, to do the thoughtful thing. It hurts to hear; I hear it still. I did call him, some, when he was really around.

Dad, I would say then. *Daddy, I miss you so much, you know?* I would practically smell his wonderful smell, man sweat and cherry pipe tobacco, right through the phone.

I miss you too, No. 1 daughter, he would say, in that sad cello voice, a tenderness that cut me. I would speak glibly and gruffly, an offhand beatnik, to cover my anguish of love.

Pop, I would say. I have to ask you some stuff. Have you got a little while?

Of course, he would say, as he always did—certainly, he would say. And heedless fool that I was in my mid-twenties—which is how old he lived to know me to be—I would launch into some diatribe, strident and smug: Nothing could surprise me. I did try to surprise *him,* however, from time to time.

One Thanksgiving Day, I called him from Hana, the hard black-lava edge of windward Maui, where Lindbergh chose to be buried, wet guava jungle, ocean booming and spraying nearly to the phone booth where I spoke. It was a collect call. My stepmother answered the phone. I could hear her lips purse, hear the sour disapproval that meant to pass for scrupulous neutrality: "Here's your father."

I wonder how long it takes a young adult to comprehend that a parent's life might be an axis of its own, a twirling sun around which a first-born daughter is but one of many orbiting moons. That her father might be bowed at the shoulders before a flickering TV screen, with the weight of the evening news. That those slumped shoulders might also be yoked by the steel-cable contempt of a second wife, whose rancor against his indulgence of his daughters took the form of long, scroll-like chore lists, written out in grimly articulate longhand, magneted to the refrigerator like proclamations for infanticide; who insisted that my father genuinely question whether he had loved his girls "not wisely but too well." We didn't just leave home, we fled it.

Just as it was tough to picture him having sex, never did I consider that my father might obsess about his own destiny, scratching at the itchy what-ifs like anyone else: Would a doctorate have earned him more money, more respect? Should he summon the nerve to ask out that knockout student? Back then, I was so self-absorbed I never noticed his affair with the gin, bunches of clear little bottles like old-time medicine flasks, stashed in the low metal files of his office or under the seat of his car. He must have felt hot with illicitness when he took furtive pulls from them—the clear fire flushing up at once, in seconds coating things with a softer glaze, rendering his voice more nasal and stinging in that Socratic querying of his classes he seemed to relish so—a deliberate jerking-the-bait ceremony drizzling bemused irony over those poor blank kids like peppered honey over popsicle sticks. Nor did I guess that toward the end, he had filled the backseat of his car with travel brochures; that he planned to use his pending sabbatical to fly to Hawaii—to see me, to see the little life I had made, apart from my burdensome Mainland identity as a charismatic professor's daughter. *I have a feeling if I don't go now, he told my stepmother, I'll never see her again. I just smell death all around me, he told her.*

He was reading to her about near-death experiences the afternoon before he died, my stepmother says. She was going to a wedding, and he to a baseball game.

She had asked him that day: Do you mind dying?

Not if I can go like *that*, he had answered, snapping his fingers.

He didn't feel like going off to the ballgame that day. But he felt he should go, he said, because the tickets had been purchased and his friends were expecting him.

The rest you can guess. He went like that. At the ballgame. I don't tell many people this because I am afraid they will laugh at the vision it conjures. But my father got his wish.

After he died, his students covered the door of his office with notes to him. Notes of gratitude, notes of love, notes of goodbye. Poetry, blessings, secrets. Sometimes just their names.

Even a hopeless smartmouth leans on her father's adoration as she grows up, shapes herself around it, is fueled and steered by it. It is the pulsing nugget of plutonium that propels her gypsy flights from plush carpets and chrome faucets, comforts that emblemized a great deal to a man raised by stern immigrants in a Brooklyn apartment. (A tunnel from right to left on the map: grandparents in at Ellis Island; grandchildren popping out the other end into fragrant fresh-cut lawns of California suburbs—grandchildren who came to long for *authentic* life, in Europe!)

Wherever I was later in the world, *whatever* I was, I warmed myself at a steady torch of love between my father and me that had pre-empted words since before I had words—since the black-and-white snapshots with scallop trim: *Little Thinker in Flapping Sunbonnet*, in which a baby girl smiles easily into the camera, tiny fingers hooked trustfully over a big man's hefted right shoulder and its galaxy of freckles, freckles and heft my own back would once match exactly.

Why, I would ask him this time, did we never, ever speak of my mother? Why did we treat her death like a form of radioactive waste, buried under years of pantomime to convince ourselves, and the world, that we were "normal"? Two little girls at eleven and nine had felt at once the leverage available in admitting we'd lost our mother, and though it spooked us to say the words, we were not above working it some. The shock in people's faces made your lips want to curl in an inexplicable, obscene urge to smile. What shamed me more was my shivering relief: It was not my father I had lost.

What do you finally think possible, I would ask him. Between men and women, I mean. Maybe we'd both have to be very old, for me to feel right asking. Because my father had appetites, see? Appetites that got him in big trouble. You could say his appetites killed our mother. If the route was circuitous, the theme was too common—a man compelled to investigate other women ("It was as if he had something to prove," recalls a friend);

a brokenhearted wife finally subsumed by her own sorrow. ("It's like a cancer," she told someone. "It grows and grows.") He spent latter years volunteering time manning suicide-prevention hot-lines. My sister and I knew nothing of the drama until years after his death—and by then it was like finding an old cache of fragile bones that are wan and blank, as stripped of blame for anyone as of the meat once on them. Or like viewing ruins of a stage on which a ghastly tragedy played out long ago, players and play now dust.

If I called him up now, I would not be heedless anymore. I'd be weighed down with my own evening news.

I'd apologize for having been so glib, so hip, so immortal. I'd ask: Do you remember the day little sister's young husband was killed in the snow? The Vietnam vet just ready to resume his life, the toboggan accident? A frozen snowbank, a broken neck; it was over in moments. She was nineteen. You came to us at once, sat down, took my little sister's entire grown-woman body into your lap in the rocking chair and rocked her while she cried, your face a clench of bewildered pain—this burnt into my vision, superimposed on the rest of our lives like an etched lens—your disbelieving voice on the phone, the wince in your words: Was he really killed, Joan? Yes, Daddy, he was, I had had to reply, out of the numb gas my body and brain had become.

Our lives eventually did unfold and walk upright. There came other lovers, marriages; there came children. But I cannot think of you in that rocking chair with your arms around your youngest girl, my weeping sister, your face having no recourse, yet plainly seeking for one, without still wanting to burrow my own head between both your laps, and make it be all right.

I go running in the park a lot now, Pop. I run past lines of cars parked along the shining lawns and trees. Eucalyptus branches thresh and glitter in the ocean wind, pointing-finger leaves flutter down on me, birds sing liquid passwords to each other. I look into the car windows I run past, partly to see my own face—to prove I'm there, thinker of these thoughts, that it is me who is running, me who owns the face in the tinted glass, more pallid in this powdery northern light, under this fine film of sweat. I look at my reflection in the glass car windows partly to see if I might still be called a pretty woman. What I really expect to see in the glass is an old basset-hound-faced professor from Brooklyn, feathers of gray hair sticking out as if just off the pillow, remnants of his breakfast drying on his tie.

If A Is A

THE ACCOUNTANT for our firm lay the ad before me on my desk. She looked very twinkly. "I know you don't believe in this anymore. But this looks like you, doesn't it?"

I glanced at it.

YOUR CHOICE OF MUSIC *tells more than you think. I'm handsome, smart, fit, and crazy for Bach, Beethoven, Mozart, Chopin, and related good guys. If you are single, slim, and nuts about these guys too, consider the implications.*

Certain of those words should have leapt out at me in neon. Most of all the ghastly, ubiquitous *slim*. Maybe I suppressed knowing better because what leapt out instead were the composers' names. I loved them so. Anyone who cited them first must be in some way worth meeting. Surely.

I thought: Nah.

I thought: Hell. At least we could talk about music for five minutes. I sat down to type.

Hello. Your ad struck me because I'm a fool for those guys.

Should we meet for a drink? His call came at work. "Do you—" he paused. "—match the other criteria in the ad?"

No, not at all, ninny. That is why I am reciting descriptions of myself like a slave on an auction block. But I answered evenly. "I don't know whether I am what you consider *slim*." I spoke the word the way you'd grasp a soiled diaper. "But I am athletic, and my body is strong and—well, womanly." I blushed, horrified. "How tall are you? What do you weigh?" Point-blank. A clinician. My stomach tightened. "Five-four. One-twenty-five." Whistle a happy tune. Make believe you're brave.

"Well, the ex-wife was five-four—she's an aerobics teacher—weighed about that." Terrific. I shook off visions of some harried, hard-bodied woman, straining to sweat this man out of her life.

Stop that. Be kind. Learn something, I commanded myself as I drove to the appointed bar after work, already feeling so furtive and conspicuous I imagined people in passing cars were smirking at me. Just another charm on the charm bracelet, I crooned to myself. Good Stories Later Told. Sense of adventure, and all that. Yet I could not stifle some small central compartment intoning: fool as I stood at the bar's entrance, squinting through smoke at the inevitable gaggle of sad souls taking private communion at the polished wood. Then I heard my name. A slender man was slipping off his barstool and removing earphones attached to a belt-clipped walkman. He looked bland, impassive. My stomach fell into itself, *boof*, a dropped soufflé. At once I knew that a sort of generic geniality was going to be the very best I could do.

We shook hands. His was thin, cool, limp. The urge to bolt inflamed me. *No escape*, I mused, forcing a tight smile at this hapless male being, hating him, sorry for him, hating myself, sorry for myself, cursing my own naiveté in falling yet again for the siren tease of the personals ads. What a heartbreakingly credulous species we are. We may be so bludgeoned by prior dating disasters that our psyches are green and purple; we stagger ahead to try again. The inherent doom of the personals, I now saw, was identical to that of the blind date: Gulp the bait—and die. To persuade oneself against an avalanche of evidence that *this time, it might work* and then face the shrieking, mocking reality was like slamming into a glass door: my whole face stung.

He was having a trendy beer. I ordered a stiff margarita—for cheer, and courage. We traded histories. He'd been a stockbroker awhile. Threw it all over one day to hit the road in a van. (I perked up.) Somewhere on that road acquired an organic cleaning-fluid business which sustains him to this day. (I wilted.) Since divorcing he has lived in an empty apartment with a shedding German shepherd who suffers hip dysplasia.

I took urgent swallows from my little blue straws.

Suddenly he brightened. Had I any idea why he had named those particular composers?

I thrust out my last, drooping hope. "Because they might reveal qualities of character, dimensions of the heart, possibly even intellect?"

His features fell. "Intellect! Ah, no, certainly not intellect." He shook his head sadly. Big cannons were being wheeled out, and I didn't know what the war was.

"No, what liking these composers reveals are certain of your basic metaphysical philosophical assumptions."

I stared at him. "Excuse me?"

He took a breath. "This is hard to describe, for those who don't see it as we do—"

"*We?*" My eyes were popping.

"—we who feel that the universe is either knowable, or

unknowable. That reality is what it is, or not. That reason and logic are fixed and real and knowable as this tabletop (he tapped it)—or this beer bottle (he seized it)—or not."

I stared.

"See, knowledge proceeds from basest to highest levels." Patient as a tutor. "Like a pyramid, or any structure. We just need to agree on the content of the building blocks." His eyes were clear, and absolutely guileless.

Suddenly I felt very tired. "Why must these immense questions about the nature of the universe be answered for you simply to *like* someone?"

He leaned forward. "Because with my next romantic partner, if we can both agree that A is A—that truth is real and knowable and constant, and arrived at through successive levels of logic and reason—then we'll get along."

He was designing a road map. A blueprint. A trail of crumbs that would lead Hansel and his new, improved Gretel out of the Black Forest. It was Relational Fail-Safe he wanted, and he was inventing it now, hand-over-hand, knife in his teeth.

He was an exotic plant, growing in twisty zigzags toward a remote light source.

"Let me see if I have this right. You want your prospective partner in effect to sign a contract, agreeing to think reality is the same thing you think it is, so you can unravel your way out of fights."

He nodded, unblinking. "My last wife thought that because she felt a thing, it was right," he said, his voice rough and distant a moment. Then he brightened. "Now, don't mistake me. Feelings are terrific; feelings are fine—as long as they proceed from an agreed-on basis of logic and reason." Eyes wide and placid. Absolute conviction.

I stood and shook his cool hand. "I . . . admire your quest."

He looked peaceful as I strode out into the sharp freeing cold.

Dragging my charm bracelet.

Hidden Assets

WHEN A PHONE CALL informed me that a tennis-ball-sized lump near my ovaries was not supposed to be there, and that there was no way of learning more except to open me up and get it, I did not react with honor.

I was shaking. If it's malignant? I asked my doctor, a petite, brilliant surgeon who awed her colleagues with her exact prognoses and cool nerve. If it's malignant, she told me in a soft but firm voice, then it, and everything else that is, will have to come out. What about babies? I asked. Can you save any ovum? Not if it's bad, she answered. Can you wake me up in the middle and tell me what's going on before you take anything out? I was begging into the phone receiver, my roaring heart drowning out the absurdity of the plea. No, she responded patiently. That is not the way it's done. We'll only take what we absolutely have to. But you must sign a release before you go under, permitting us to take out whatever we feel we must to save your life.

The word too dreadful to name was *hysterectomy*. I was 37,

single, childless, and not at all ready for the motherhood option to expire.

I looked at Cindy. She looked at me. She was beside me when the call came. A beat earlier we'd been chatting over coffee, fretting over daily trivia; two women so unquestionably whole and well that neither of us thought of anything in terms of "whole" or "well." The next moment I found myself bidding in a gruesome auction, bartering portions of my reproductive organs like poker chips with a doctor who refused to bet. But here's the thing. At the moment I'd asked whether any eggs could be saved, Cindy whispered, *I'll carry them for you.*

The morning of the operation, the rest of the world went to school and work and tended its kids. My friend took time off from her job and drove me to the hospital. It was very early; neither of us had slept. We plopped down on a waiting room couch, watched morning talk shows. Bleary, Cindy nevertheless kept me talking, about anything—celebrity gossip, office problems, her day's plans. The mindless chatter was a kind of pact, and though dazed with fear, I was lucid enough to feel very grateful. We both knew about the percentage of accidental deaths from reactions to anaesthesia. We both strove to keep our eyes away from the families who were waiting for news of loved ones, many sleeping on the couches, others in a kind of catatonia before the droning televisions. Every so often an exhausted physician would step into the room, still in full operating gear, to confer with them in low tones. When my name was called, Cindy and I embraced, and she waved at me the entire time I walked to the elevator to the operating room. I looked back one last time from the elevator, and there was her waving hand, in the far distance.

When I woke, in a green haze of nausea and pain, the first image I could bring into focus was—Cindy, applying chapstick to what must have been my cracked green lips. The tumor was benign, everything had gone splendidly, and now I had only to heal. The day I was able to go home, she had her car outside waiting. At my apartment, she had filled my refrigerator with good food and juice, and by my bed, piled some fat paperbacks. She phoned every day to praise my progress—I could walk two blocks, three blocks, ten, twenty. And as the routine rhythms of our lives settled back in place, she never ceased her regular roundelay of meals and drinks bought, counsel dispensed, luggage loaned, furious defenses hurled at real or imagined enemies. Cindy is a fortress, and as her friend, I am its beloved and sovereign citizen.

This level of attention can be perceived as tyrannical and intrusive, and she knows it, and we've talked about it. I can only feel thankful. To me Cindy is a "pick-up-pieces" friend. This is the one who collects all the jagged shards some grim fate has left of you—gather up every last one, take them home, and patiently try to reassemble them. The one who will jump in the car and drive over at once. The one who takes time on the phone to listen, and responds in ways that make sense. The one who says, yes, of course, come over and eat with us; we'll wait for you. It's easy to praise in hindsight, of course; easy to wax sappy over when glasses are raised—but staggering to witness in action, in the midst of busy life. Why? Because it is such a marvel of generosity in a world where most people are annoyed even to have to briefly delay their own self-absorbed orbits. A pick-up-pieces friend is good for bottom-line, twenty-four-hour, whatever-it-takes faith; whether it's money, a bed, food, physical or mental first aid. I am convinced we simply cannot know what this means until we need it, and receive it. Earthquake, fire, cancer and AIDS victims may have a good idea.

This is the thing that women do. For those of us who exist apart from conventional families, who live circumscribed routines unalleviated by larger community, who inhabit one tiny cell in the giant honeycombs that form a city—and even for those tucked into conventional networks, with safety nets strung below them—women coming to women's aid forms a palpable security in a world going madder by the minute, real as any Individual Retirement Account or certificate of deposit. It's a kind of insurance we don't want to lean on too often, but are passionately glad to have.

I worry sometimes that I can never properly reciprocate, because of our economic differences, but Cindy waves these words away. And I do not want to dishonor her, or us, by framing the relationship in terms of matching deed for deed—to reduce it to a scorecard or competition. After the surgery I told her I could not understand all she had done for me; that I had never been cared for that way before. "It's the way I was raised," she shrugged. She's from Minnesota.

Early Exits

FIRST HEARD OF HER through a young friend who had taken her creative writing class.

"She'd show up drunk a lot, and often drugged as well," he reported. "It was prescribed stuff; she had a real bad palsy in her arms. She'd tell us she was sorry, hold down her hand, go off and take some pills. When she was just on the medication," he added, "she was a little more alert. When she was drunk *and* on medication, it was kind of pointless to listen to her." Two years later, my friend remembered, "She'd just published a book of short stories; it had been well received. She was inebriated; had a hard time putting words together. The class just kind of sat there; after a while everybody left.

"At that moment," my friend recalled, "the chairman of the department walked in. He took her aside. I waited for her. She came back, and he had just fired her." My friend decided to help her home. "She tried to tell me she could get on a bus, but I told her I was going to drive her." My friend drove the writer home, and saw her to her door. "She thanked me, and walked in. It was the last time I saw her."

When my friend told me this story, I did not ask for particulars because I could see them too easily; the unsteady woman before a roomful of uneasy students, her glassy eyes and thick speech in apparent contradiction to the solid body of acclaimed work behind her. Oddly, the description of her drunken pathos attracted me to this woman, though I'd never read her work. I was intrigued by the peculiar bald honesty and even gallantry some-how implicit in a bright, accomplished woman's acceding to the obliterating ether of drink or drugs.

That's right: honesty and gallantry.

There is a silent mandate in our culture to put up a busy, if membrane-fragile, front against the despair most thoughtful people feel now and again: despair for the brevity of beauty, for injustice and suffering in the world, for hypocrisy, for loneliness. Despair that whispers behind our minds as if it were cellular memory—a progressive, melancholic awareness built into our bodies, timed to release at maturation, like the onset of pubescence. But by the time we're grown we are so locked into a tacit code of manners that only some children, "crazies," drunks, and junkies can face—or name—certain truths. There's a shocking purity about it; an in-your-face splash when someone declares that things are not fine, thanks—and that there is no fast fix for what is wrong.

This is by no means a defense of addiction. Rather, I mean to point out that when any woman or man capitulates to the anesthetizing refuge of pills or alcohol, some element in those of us who have lived as long must silently resonate: *yes, I know.*

A year or so after hearing my friend's story I noticed in newspaper reviews that the woman's latest novel had been received kindly, if not to thunderous praise; at least it had got the kind of genial nod many writers would kill for. I felt glad that for all her personal trouble, the woman was continuing to produce, and getting good feedback for it. When I saw she was to speak to a local writers' group, I arrived early—eager to get a firsthand sense of who she was, how she was, what made her tick. Little as I knew of her, what I did know pulled at me—some fancied combination of poignancy and grit.

She was a tall, pale, big-boned woman; handsome, quietly well-dressed; her skin had that translucent fragility that signals a delicate and troubled being living behind it. A slight young man guided her in by the elbow; he seemed to be on hand to ensure her physical and psychic safety, as if she were a skittish colt or a priceless piece of china. Her smile was nervous, hopeful, overbright. She looked into people's faces, nodded, smiled that crinkling smile: only her eyes betrayed a distant sensibility. There was a graciousness about her, and a sad bravado.

She waited alone out on the terrace of the house while the audience gathered inside. I glanced through the window to see her sitting in the sun with a cigarette, looking absently past the green leaves of the garden—and immediately I looked away, pained by the softness of the scene: her placid patience, the afternoon sunlight dappling her like a blessing. While we waited, I picked up a copy of her first novel, turning it over to look at her photograph. Gazing out was a girl who appeared to be barely twenty. Her young face mesmerized me—expectant, smooth; clear eyes posing hard questions, eager to engage. I looked back at the woman in the garden: she was glassy, shell-shocked, yet still gallant; willing to wait out there to go through with this.

Suddenly I knew that the gossip and details of her life were unimportant. We've all heard it before; known much of it ourselves—the litany a friend calls sociogenic: childhood abuse, tragic love affairs, loss, abandonment. It was when the novelist spoke of her characters—how she knew their entire lives before citing them on paper; how they came to her; how she felt them interact—it was then that the woman came alive, *present* among us: inhabiting the situation and herself; assuming clear, no-nonsense command.

When I said goodbye, in a sudden fit of shyness I could only take her hand and say, "Thank you." She looked at me as if she were genuinely hoping I'd say more. I fled into the warm afternoon with a guilty sense of relief, making a beeline for the home of good friends who would feed me dinner. We would play with their baby, drink wine, laugh a lot. I did not sense this woman had that kind of restorative warmth to go back to.

One month later the novelist was found dead in her home. Whether it was deliberate or not would never be clear. What was clear was that her body had finally succumbed to years upon years of excess. My first thought—an angry stab—was I *should have anticipated this*. (If I could not have somehow prevented her death, then I should have been braced for it. But how?) Second thought: That could be me. That could be lots of us. She was single, she lived alone, she wrote, she was only forty-three years old. She routinely softened her days and nights with substances proven, at least for a while, to work.

As I read the obituary I felt a funny voyeuristic tingle: I'd just shaken her hand, laughed at her jokes, looked into her eyes. There is a kind of sizzling charge in the mere proximity to a light that only just went out, and one feels ashamed of the subtle tremors of pleasure to have been among the last witnesses—ashamed of one's relief to have escaped the same voiding. At the memorial service someone read a poem actually envisioning the woman's body on the cold steel of the morgue table, the identification tag on the big toe. You wanted to cry out against the indignity of the image, even while stunned by its blunt truth.

But people then spoke of how this woman was in fact a "winner" more *because* of her obvious struggles than despite them. They cited the courage of her ability to joke about her body's decline; the real generosity of her managing to be a good friend and teacher "from the middle distance," despite the pain that must have howled in her inner ear at splitting volume, day and night.

Then we all wandered off, back to our lives' daily rounds. Now I go about those rounds with the pieces of her story rumbling in my head, like low thunder. When someone dies, we come to accept that the relentless commerce of life will swallow up the incident; that those who care, however terribly, will finally move on. But when that death is a suicide—conscious or cumulative—it makes a deep mark on our memory's scoreboard: another soul decided to let go early; to follow that siren lure to release. And anyone who's lived awhile, and who denies ever having heard that siren lure, is either a fool or a liar, or has lived a life out of TV sitcoms.

It is the tension between the temptation of letting go and the deals we strike with ourselves in the interim that arrests me—particularly among those of us who live solitary lives: perhaps because we seem most easily able to simply disengage, to float away. The deals we strike don't always match the lists of responsibilities recited by the well-meaning, or the frightened, or the pious. It may be art or work or family that prods people to go on. Mercifully, it is more often plain curiosity. "Save death for last," a local musician advised a depressed friend. "It comes anyway."

But there are times, for some, when none of these arguments proves weighty enough. And when this happens, all our anguish and anger notwithstanding, we must ultimately respect it. Because by now we know better than not to. Save your pity or disdain; save your higher moral ground. Let those who've so chosen, have their early exit. Let them go to their true ease.

Be's That Way

WITNESS the competent, prudent woman conducting a perfectly plausible, even distinguished life, meet a man who attracts her, who is kind, smart, and good. And see her, upstanding citizen, marvel of comely savvy, proceed to fall apart.

Her body melts. Her good brains shudder and implode. She mutates before her own eyes into someone with all the sense and poise and critical judgment of a toddler at naptime. For me, for a time there, one kind word or expression of interest from the nice man—and out from my bared chest, Alien-style, would burst my bloody, fibrillating heart. It would thrust itself at the astonished fellow, quivering. Here! I'd hear myself telling the hapless male, whose eyes were bulging. Take it! Take my life. Take it now.

Is it any wonder the poor man would back off, stammering that he just remembered something really, really important he had to do? "Taxi!" And he'd vanish, and I'd be left standing on the sidewalk, a thin stream of heart-juice trickling over the curb into the gutter.

What in Sam Hill was going on in there? Did I really think so little of myself? Get a grip, I'd tell the wanton heart so willing to punch out the first nice guy in sight with all its force. Count your blessings, I'd command it again and again. Name every good thing you have. Friends. Work. Health. You've got a good life, damn it. You don't have to suck one out of some guy's jugular vein.

In my ear, my lonely heart snapped back. It's not a crazy thing to want to be loved and held, to want a loving someone to see movies with, trade dreams with, even share the bathroom in the morning with.

But after a certain span of years, single women begin to see that the odds for achieving that kind of coziness may be dimming. Our peers, likeliest candidates for that level of partnership, are encumbered now, enmeshed in complicated lives sown some time ago. And while we still have faith that random events pop through the statistical net, we begin to see we'd do well to invent other ways to meet those needs for affection and companionship. Sublimate, we're told. See a therapist. Get a massage. Do things.

We do. But it doesn't seem to fix the gushing hole in the emotional armature, where an ocean of longing pours through whenever we face a kind, attractive man. If we were a submarine, we'd be sunk. Why do we place such disproportionate expectations and hopes on a man, merited or not? Aren't we wiser in the '90s? Isn't our time more precious now than to squander a second more of it on a country-western level of self-pity?

Every indication is that women still carry the tendency to give too much too soon, like a latent virus, and that we deal with that impulse—and the reality of living without men—in different ways. Some women get religion, art, or politics. Some work out 'til they're hard as steel. Some get drunk. Some go to the movies. Others get drunk *while* they're at the movies. This helps them to cry, which is hard for strong women to allow, and therefore a big relief.

Still others try taking a dim-bulb lover purely for the relief of having sex. Physical contact will bring solace, they imagine, without complications of a full-blown relationship. The flaw with this reasoning becomes clear the minute Big Hunk opens his mouth. "Hey, you sure got a lot of books here!" "Are these gray hairs?" Big, dead-end silences. No solace.

Some women agree to long-term affairs with married men: discreet, reliable, comforting. If the principals claim they are happy, one can only wish them well. But something seems forsaken. Is it simply old fairy-tale ideals of romance? Or the notion of ongoing, imperfect, risky one-on-one? Is the missing element one of sustained adventure?

For the rest of us, in any case, it ain't restful—becoming an idiot before men. Wearied to the bone, one longs to be done with it—wants to stop wanting. The most realistic prescription may be Germaine Greer's, in her recent book, *The Change.* Her message is ultimately eastern, existential: Face what is, she advises, and as best you can, take hold of it. Fix what you can, and drop-kick the rest. If lovers and husbands are woven through the tapestry of our lives like twinkling filaments, lovely. If not, it be's that way, as an old friend used to put it. Strenuous, painful—and essential to accept if we are to keep sane.

"View yourself with a kind of compassionate humor for the next ten years," suggests another friend, kindly. Greer tells us it gets easier. The sentient soul that lived many good years before the sexual and reproductive urges kicked in—and will live many good years after—must rise to answer those urges: Sorry, dear. Different life now.

But that life unfurls as no less a miracle. Given the true riches of health and friendship, work and love seem like frosting.

Because now is when we sense along our very skin the shiver of comprehension, as writer Martin Amis noted, that death is not a rumor.

Stuff the pulsing heart back in, pull the coat tighter, and go for a long walk, breathing deep.

Sailing Away

*E*LLEN B. always had the right words. Sometimes I copied them down on little scraps of paper, keeping them tucked in odd spots where I knew I would later run across them. They would clear my head and make me smile.

"No one has certainty."

"It doesn't matter about the others."

"It's just another thing in all the stuff there is."

When I despaired of ever feeling like I really had a life, she would suggest that I envision myself on one side of a very high wall. There were good things, she swore, very real good things on the other side—I just couldn't see them yet. And she told me I would run smack into those good things when I least expected to, as I rounded a street corner one day. Foolish as it may sound, this little parable made sense to me, and comforted me deeply. And yes, good things did come.

We were in our mid-thirties then. In a world of women marrying and cranking out babies as if their lives depended on it,

I rushed to Ellen for reassurance that I, in my rather monkish routine of office work and writing, was still as legitimate and worthy as all those brides and mommies. I was also recovering from an apocalyptic love affair that trailed blood off into the horizon. Most of my time was spent huddling with books and papers in an apartment furnished like a set from *La Boheme*. As she moved into editing and I into writing, I grew to feel desperately close to her, because she was one of the smartest, kindest, most thoughtful women I had ever known—and because we were among the last single, childless women we knew on Earth.

She was a tall, big-boned and graceful woman, with a face like a Modigliani painting—pale, intense, almost abstract features that held you completely—and a great joyful laugh. Over weekly dinners we'd laugh helplessly at our lives and loves, or lack of them. At how hard it was to be a woman on her own. "Let's know each other till we're old," we'd swear.

Then one winter she met someone. In a year or two they were living together; in another, married. I was part of the simple ceremony in a cabin in the rainy woods. Both bride and groom wept a little as they repeated the vows. I wept a little, too. I've lost her, I thought. Lost her to the cozy world of twos.

Still, I did not mean to allow her to vanish completely. We had to plan it more carefully, but I was still able to kidnap her away for an occasional dinner. One day when I phoned, she sounded distracted and strange. Finally I asked her what it was. There was the briefest pause. Then she said, slowly, with amazement, "I'm pregnant, Joanie."

My heart froze. Ellie and I had always known she would likely never have children. The situations for doing it had never even been close to reasonable. There had been an abortion when she was very young; her new husband was certain he did not want children. To choose him was to agree to forgo them. After some deep and anguished soul-searching, she had relented, and they had just commenced what I called their "good little life." Decent jobs. Nice home. Camping, travel.

Then, this cosmic prank. They appeared to be a couple almost carved from the serenity and autonomy and, yes, the certain amount of fussy self-indulgence associated with childlessness. I assumed she would get an early abortion to honor their agreement, and continue the life they'd planned. But she was of no such mind.

"I can't not have this baby, Joanie," she said. "It is like something life has handed me, and this time I have a situation in which I don't necessarily have to hand it back." She paused to find the words. "I don't have the heart to hand it back. I have a sense that if I *don't* do this, when I'm fifty I will feel it was just plain dumb."

"But what about Andrew?" I asked. "He may leave you."

"If he finds he has to go away because of this, then I guess he will have to go away," she said, as astonished as I was to hear the words marching out of her mouth.

Once the pregnancy was under way, she reasoned, perhaps her man would begin to feel the pull of it, the irrestible unity of it, like the moon on the tides. I could hear in her voice the shifting of allegiances already in motion. As her body prepared for its new passenger, she was making her mind ready to accommodate a massive realignment with the future.

She was also sensitive to the effect of this news on me. She knew I had a history like hers, where continuing an accidental pregnancy years ago would have meant a lifetime of sorrow for all the principals. She knew I'd spent much time coming to terms with this grief, and with the fact that, given my age and the odds, I would likely never have kids. Now she was going over to the other side.

Or the alliance would have to be reinvented.

I knew this was a moment in our friendship where the tough had damn well better get going. She was soon going to need me in a way that would make our furtive little dinners together look like "Mr. Rogers' Neighborhood." Horrific visions of single motherhood whirled in my mind: the ceaseless clawing and scrambling for money, for food, clothing, health care, child care—and overshadowing this, fatigue, loneliness, guilt.

But Ellen functioned placidly in the world, working, growing larger, quietly preparing the nest. We continued our dinners as if everything were the same. But of course nothing was the same. As she got bigger she started to think and talk differently: about childbirth methods, doctors and midwives, baby clothes, memories of her childhood and of her own mother.

Her belly was smooth and warm and luminous, like a bright moon, and she carried it the way women admire, high and centered and round. I was moved and amazed by the wisdom of my friend's forty-two-year-old body, and by her shy pride in it.

But her husband was not at all amazed. He was horrified. As far as he was concerned, the happy life he had envisioned for the two of them had been aborted before it had even begun. They lived in an uneasy stasis, and none of us knew what would happen. He loved her, but he could not love their pending child. With him, she cried, sympathized, was disgusted—but mostly just quietly went on with things. He might leave. *She would do this.* Resolutely she prepared herself for birth and motherhood alone, if need be.

During the final weeks some of her friends came together to give her an "anti-shower." I christened it that because we were women who normally did not enjoy the squealy atmosphere of baby showers. Most of us were childless, most acclimated to it. But we all loved Ellen. And so when she remarked, just before the shower, that she felt very frightened, I didn't understand.

"Of labor pain? Of something going wrong?"

"No," she said sadly. "Frightened of the fact that I feel like I am getting into a little boat and sailing away from all the rest of you, waving goodbye."

I shivered. Until now we'd all been in the same little boat: childless by choice or default. Now she was going away, to that other great and hallowed dimension of Mothers. Maybe I was kidding myself; maybe I was losing her forever. From a tightened throat, I poured out reassurances that I would not let her set sail alone. But in my heart I was not so sure anyone could really do that. My own self-absorbed existence by comparison suddenly felt insubstantial, puny with squirming little vanities and delusions. A plate of worms.

What is it that stabs us so about "losing" a friend in this way? Is it about abandonment, as when a childhood pal moves away? Is it the sense of betrayal that, say, Peter Pan felt when he returned to find Wendy grown up one day? (She tells him: "I couldn't help it, Peter.")

At the same time, the reasons for abstaining from mother-hood are never easy to acknowledge. Considered in soft-focus abstract (watching families in the park), the urge of it can still yank hard. But after-images of grittier realities—bills, absence of a helping partner, a cramped apartment and flimsy paycheck that barely buys food, let alone child care—these make a single woman shiver.

Still, at the "anti-shower" I fidgeted as people congratulated me on recent stories published. The real miracle, the true creator, sat luminous beside me with her luscious big belly high and perfect in her lap. She never looked more beautiful; light seemed to seep from her. Opening gifts, she cracked: "You thought you knew me, right? But suddenly I'm yelling things like, 'Receiving blankets—

thank God!' and you're wondering, who is this really?" She was still her, baby or no.

We decided that she is the astronaut exploring one kind of deep and mysterious space, reporting back about what it's like out there. And when I write, exploring another kind of mysterious space, I will report to her what it's like, in there. And I will end this account before any of us yet knows who will be born, or how we all did with it.

After all, no one has certainty. And this is just another thing, in all the stuff there is.

In Tears We Trust

ONDAY MORNING in the waking city. Birds warbling on the wire, children swinging lunchboxes, sun spilling over rooftops.

Out the door, cup of caffeine in hand. Rain last night: clean air, new week. Walk a block to the car. Place the briefcase and coffee on the passenger seat. Shut the door. Step off the sidewalk to walk to the driver's side—and feel those tiny corrugations on the soles of your boots, meant to supply necessary traction on wet pavement, fail.

Your feet fly out from under you and you land, somehow, on your knees, shredding the skin which had so seamlessly adorned them a moment before. Blood and pain. Many bad words. Incredulity. Stagger into the car, moaning with pain, start it, and take it down the street to idle closer to your front door while you race back up your apartment stairs to change, each thump stabbing a knee. And as you gaze out the window, fresh clothing in hand, you see the meter maid alongside your vehicle writing out an

38

expensive ticket. You have parked it on the street-cleaning side, exactly thirty seconds before the sweeper is due. You race downstairs barefoot, gasping. "I thought the streetsweeper had already come and gone!"

She looks at you with more contempt than you thought any human capable. "Well, he hasn't," she purrs in the acid condescension reserved for morons, and glides away.

So began my Monday.

I trudged back up my stairs, and as I sat down on the toilet lid with a bottle of hydrogen peroxide, something cracked inside me, and I began to cry. Deep sobs, pouring tears. I couldn't stop. And as I wept and wept, I felt mystified, and thought: *What right have you to cry?* So you hurt yourself. So you got a ticket. Big deal! You eat well, sleep warm and dry, love your friends and work. Paraplegics have a right to cry! Single mothers on welfare have a right to cry! But you—healthy, whole, solvent citizen, not in jail, not at war—are in no position to feel entitled to cry.

So why did I cry? I asked around.

"Your tissues were softened," said the local massage therapist. "Collagen was rushing to the injury site after you fell and your body had softened to let it move there fast, sending water to the eye."

"The time of the month," someone at the office suggested. "The alignment of the stars," said another.

My sister knew in a heartbeat. She has three little sons, and they live in the country. She knows everything about breakdowns. She knows about the groceries falling out of the car, the dog dragging home a deer carcass—antlers and all—the baby screaming, the phone ringing, saucepan boiling over, mail splattering into the mud, the older boys fighting. All at once.

It isn't so much what happens, she says, as that it happens all at once. Distresses add up, over time, so that when you finally break, you break from accrued weight. But it goes deeper.

At a certain point, said my wise sister, "You cry for ev-erything." Everything that ever happened. And she's right. I cried because my parents were dead, and I missed them. I cried for lost love—that I felt so alone. I cried because I felt overwhelmed by futility: pushing and pushing to keep things rolling, appear clean and presentable, get places on time, dodge evil, sidestep danger, stay clear of the streetsweeper—to meet the most minimal expec-tations in the commerce of life—then watch helplessly as the slightest lapse of attention dissipates these efforts, and the giant rock rolls right back down over you like the one that came after Indiana Jones in *Raiders of the Lost Ark.*

The other part of crying was, I felt reduced to a child again. I would have laughed at the scene if it still hadn't hurt so much— perched on the lid of the toilet, snuffling, dabbing at my bloody (discoloring, swelling) knees with hydrogen peroxide. Remember-ing when there was someone kneeling at my knees, saying things to make it better. Remembering secret pride in the bruises and scabbing I would show off later. Remembering spray-on Bactine, Campho-Phenique, the surgical adhesive smell of Band-Aids. Remembering feeling entitled to cry. Entitled, hell—kids have carte blanche.

But it's so difficult for strong women to cry. So fiercely have we steeled ourselves, so deeply is the instinct tamped down, it can get lost. We've steeled ourselves even though we are told it's far healthier to induce tears with any trick—maudlin music, sappy movies, television—than to let anger and sadness collect in the psyche like a boil. When the reflex to weep kicks in unexpectedly, touched off by a small mishap or a Rube Goldberg series of them, it can feel baffling. Crying is for tragedies, we've told ourselves.

Though I didn't allow myself to trust it at first, how good it felt to cry. To be sidelined for a spell; out of the contest. To give up—even briefly. I was tired and empty, subdued as I dressed again. I put the parking ticket in a drawer. I walked downstairs slowly, and back out again into the city streets, dragging the armor of grown-womanness along with me. I'd put it on again, later.

Just then it would have banged my knees.

Sins of Omission

A FRIDAY NIGHT PARTY: office people, friends of office people, friends of friends. The crowd spanned all strata. One beautiful young woman was half-Czech, half-Egyptian. Nice apartment; plenty of food and drink; good, blaring music propelling things into that happy, chaotic, forward momentum. My expectations of the evening were mild: to eat, drink, chat up a few familiar faces, perhaps a few new ones. Maybe I'd dance a time or two.

These things I did. Then I spotted an interesting man talking with a close friend of mine, so I walked over and introduced myself. He had shambly good looks, humor and intelligence in his eyes, a calm, relaxed manner. He looked to be near my age, not too tall or thin, not too anything. Comfortable, like a soft pair of slippers.

We began to trade backgrounds and, to my delight, shared many tastes and opinion: music, books, film, cities, careers. He seemed to appreciate my ready understanding of his habits and ideas, and I felt he affirmed my own. I was enchanted. It's rare to find such connection anywhere, and my tongue and spirits were pleasantly loosened by champagne. It was so noisy where we stood that we had to shout, so we found a quieter spot in an upstairs room, where we proceeded to talk at great and earnest length.

In the course of this talk, I began to feel there might be a possible attraction blooming between us. His posture got more casual as the talk deepened, and I allowed mine to echo his. And though he made no overt gesture, said nothing untoward or overfamiliar, in the course of our vibrant, exploratory conversation, I found him wonderfully attentive, thoughtful, curious, wise, and funny. In short, all the right stuff.

He described his life in this city to me: his job, his apartment, his car, his computer, sound equipment, problems, speculations. An intelligent bachelor's life. He seemed to truly enjoy his work and hobbies, having arrived at them through considerable trial and error—and I of course related all the genealogies of mine. He looked directly into my eyes, smiled the softest smile. Though I swear I had no sense of what might reasonably be expected to happen next, I did not then much actually care. Champagne makes you much more willing to live in the moment, I suppose. But I was thrilled to be finding such connection with such a lovely man. "Heated agreement," a friend calls it. I was glowing.

Our talk went on for more than an hour, and we had ignored all the (by now plentiful and raucous) partyers converging around us. We'd gotten to a point in the discussion where we were deep into a comparative analysis of various movies. Both our glasses were nearly empty.

He took a breath. "I have a three-year-old daughter," he said, looking at me strangely—tentatively, sort of sideways—"and everything is Disney, Disney, Disney."

I could see his face registering my shock. "You do?" I

sputtered after a beat's delay. I fought to collect myself. Well: He is a divorced or separated dad, then. Nothing strange about that. Say something. "Where does your little girl stay? I mean, where's her mom?" I chirped, thinking he would say the name of another state, or town, or at least another neighborhood.

"Here with me," he answered, and again he was looking at me in that queer, sidelong way. Only now that sidelong look had become clearly identifiable. It was a hangdog, sheepish look. "Her mom's here, tonight, around here somewhere." He nodded toward the revelers around us, then back at me, very sheepish now as he said, slowly, "My brother and his wife agreed to babysit tonight."

I stared at the man. The champagne, and all the bubbling words and ideas that had swirled around us euphorically for the previous hour, seemed to have evaporated with no trace. After a pause, I managed to stammer what I hoped was a logical response. But I can assure you I was a stunned and shaken woman in that moment, and that man would have had to have been brain dead not to know it.

He looked at his empty glass, then at me: hangdog, bordering on sly. The jig, as they say, was up. I toasted him with my own empty glass, a weak attempt at a caustic "touché." In a flat voice I said, "Time?"

"Time," he nodded. In his eyes I saw he knew very well what he had done, and that he knew I knew. We spoke not another word.

We rose and went downstairs, in single file. My brain was roaring. I moved at once to the drinks table and tried to lose myself in more alcohol, in noisy greetings with friends. During the next minutes I caught a glimpse or two of him moving past. Around his lips played a look that I will never forget: trying for grave sobriety, but over this, irrepressibly, amused and pleasured by a secret triumph. And I hated him then. Equal parts hate, hurt and abject confusion. I drank too much, and wandered home in a baffled, anguished stupor.

During the (painfully hung-over) days that followed, I went over and over the sequence of events in my mind. Where had I taken a wrong turn? I consider myself able to read people fairly well. What should I have done differently? Been more skeptical? Risked less? Was I crazy? Overly needy? Hypersensitive? Why did I feel like my guts had been suctioned out?

I finally decided: I may have been foolishly overeager. But what should have happened, should have happened very early. When we spoke of where we lived. "I live with my wife and child," this man should have told me then. It may have been awkward. But it would have permitted us both the chance to salvage, or invent, something honest. Something built on the known: what a friend calls "the dignity of fact."

Perhaps this man still carries in his mind the memory of that night. Most likely he has long forgotten it. I will not forget. There are sins of commission, as the saying goes, and sins of omission. Though no laws were broken, no visible bruises or bloodstains as evidence in court, what that man did that night was wrong. As wrong as any wrong can ever be.

The worst of it is, I don't think it's an uncommon story.

Just Wages

BEFORE WE had jobs, for most of us, school was the job. And dread of the job began early: What kid has not scrinched her mind tight, trying to boil her body temperature to fever-level to gain a day off—see how that day unfurled, apart from the already-routine dressing and toting, the marching off to a lifetime of dressing and toting? What kid, after the delicious shock of encountering *Huck Finn*, did not float on dreams of river rafting and sleeping in caves, with not a nanosecond's thought to classrooms papered with correct handwriting and electric bells shrilling the time? School was the beginning of Duty, and most of us managed to fall forward through it—some of us falling out, or off, before others. But eventually we shouldered the larger duty, got a social security number, and went off looking for work.

I have worked since I was seventeen, and in that time have done many things, from cleaning apartments to teaching in the Peace Corps. Before I determined that my work was to write (which I hasten to add, almost never obviates a "real job") I took what jobs I could, and saw the whole business as rather a whimsi-cal challenge. I thought of myself as a sort of gypsying Margaret Mead, each job a charm on the anthropologist's bracelet, the weirder or more exotic, the better. Things got less whimsical as I got older, of course, more mindful of time, energy, and my own dearest needs. James Agee lamented the difficulty of finding a paying niche he could stand: "In the long run I suspect that the fault . . . is in me . . . that I hate any job on earth, as a job and hindrance and semi-suicide." Who has not felt it?

But I seldom had a choice. Churning madly across that huge pool of the American work force called the "service" sector, I have been a salesclerk, waitress, maid, test-tube washer, secretary, tutor, typesetter. I've filed library cards and swept sidewalks. I've tended a gas-station—read the entire *Sherlock Holmes* series in between dropping people's money into a safe. I have served cocktails and edited books, sorted fruit in a canning factory. I was an au pair. Ran a resume service. Weighed babies, passed out anti-malarial drugs, taught the concept of germs causing disease. I've done some things that were a bit unsavory, but I have not turned tricks, unless you mean metaphorically—which some people think any job amounts to. I remember the day one bitter employer, the lone male editor on a small newspaper, yelled: "All jobs are a form of whoring, and the sooner you learn that, the better." (Our all-female staff was striking and forming a union at the time. We got our demands met, and then we all quit, sickened by the enmity of the experience. But none of us regretted what we had learned. And it was not about whoring.)

Much later, in an essay called "What Receptionists Know," I poured out the mind-numbing list of diplomatic and mothering skills that position requires. I called the work a hybrid of the Red Cross and the State Department; a dessert topping and a floor wax. The person operating Mission Control gladhands VIPs, counsels pregnant colleagues, mediates for divorced ones, orders pizza, smooths the way in every conceivable aspect (some near-inconceivable). It was a great relief to tell—greater still to be answered by the warm chorus of female readers (even one man) who said, *yes: you got it right.* For the sad fact remains that Human Factor work, featuring actual warmth, finely tuned discretion, and care, is still performed in the overwhelming majority by women, and still slogs along—like motherhood—least valued and least paid. Though women tend not to define themselves as much in terms of their jobs as men do, people still tend to ask *what do you do* before they ask other things, and even the goofiest, most provisional task still takes up the biggest part of our waking lives. We are what we do.

Yet *I need the money* is a bottom line no one argues, and we fill ourselves to bloating with fantasies of the blissful freedom of the rich. I have had enough traffic with people of means now, though, to observe their very real and singular problems. It is no secret that support groups operate in this country for the ranks of the wealthy, from lottery winners to families of very old money, and it is no secret (nor funny) that these people, though they "gain the whole world," indeed often suffer real crises of meaning: They desire, in effect, an authentic desire. Put another way, the measure of a life seems to boil down to how it feels first thing on waking. John Steinbeck supposedly said, "A man puts his pants on in the morning to go *do* something," and this impulse plays no favorites. Once, as a secretary for a group of attorneys, I greeted a new partner in the firm whom I happened to know came from sizeable wealth. He had everything—literally did not need to work; why was he bothering? He looked me straight in the eye: "I need to feel useful."

But that is not quite all of it. Women have for some time been keenly aware of their "usefulness," right up to the moment they simply lay down and died of it. The most vital corollary of usefulness would seem to be its meaningful acknowledgement. People need to know their work is honored, from toilet-scrubbers to heads of state—and to me this means being named, thanked in a context that makes sense, and paid decently. I have always thought it strange that those at the top of employment pyramids often did least, had it easiest, and were paid most—strange because they did not appear that terribly much smarter than anyone else. Mine was the inverse of an old equation: *If you're rich, why aren't you smart?* Some intangible was being rewarded, and when I was younger I could not always discern what that was. Now warier and wearier, I know it was often political savvy, which is not the kind of smart I meant, nor much admire. Perhaps the question should have been, *why aren't you wise?*

Even the very young need to feel they are getting up for a reasonable reason, that the world they go to meet is wise enough to cherish and reward its human factor; perhaps it is especially the very young who need to know this. And that is one reason, alongside what I have known and seen of work, that I am not smirking when I read that the Clinton administration ponders how to help implement a "politics of meaning," beginning with the honoring of labor—all labor. Why not at least place the language before people's eyes, even for a day? Why not.

No One Escapes

*I*T IS a professional office which shall remain nameless, populated by startlingly beautiful, well-educated, accomplished young women. We asked these luminous beings in their early twenties, who have caring lovers, who thrive at their work, who appear to be zipping the world crisply into their briefcases: What is your greatest obsession? What are you most hung up about?

The answer reported to me by my polltakers was unanimous, and it made me slump down over my desk like a kid assigned to copy out the *Encyclopedia Brittanica*. The women we polled are afraid of the following things, in this order: getting old, ugly, and—presumably as a direct consequence of sins One and Two—having no one to love them. Running a long fourth came natural and man-made disasters.

Dear God, I thought. No one escapes.

The formal address Ms. may be common courtesy. The nation may boast an administration whose first lady, you will pardon the expression, kicks ass. Opportunities flourish and less crap is tolerated than ever before, yet smart young women like the above still think this way. Movies like *Basic Instinct* still clean up at the box office, and magazines still teem with recast images of Barbie, or Barbarella. As *The Beauty Myth* author Naomi Wolf put it, women's magazine covers feature Claudia Schiffer, while those of worldlier journals feature "some nondescript middle-aged white guy, because he still owns it all." Public depictions of women still tend to remain rigid and narrow—about the size of a coffin, say.

Perhaps the single worst thing about being caught in the youth-and-beauty battle, as any female over age ten will tell you, is its apparent endlessness: a dragon eating its own tail. Never can you flush it completely from awareness, never can you be done with it. A heroin habit might be easier to purge: once licked, it has better odds of staying gone. Even if you do manage to forge yourself into a mirror-copy of Claudia Schiffer—you poor mortal, you must be more vigilant than Paul Revere to maintain it. Do the thousand and one necessary things to keep it hard and shiny and, above all, never drop guard. One small lapse could trigger a series of them, and before you know it you will be at the bottom of the hill again: old and ugly, with no one loving you.

I have a girlfriend who once posed for herself a perverse little riddle. If she had to choose between them, which would she rather have: a coveted doctoral degree, or thinness for life? This is a teacher, writer, and mother, wise, beautiful, of normal and graceful size—who prizes literary wisdom so much that for a time she was getting up at 4 A.M. to study to achieve that degree. She allows, of course, that women with Ph.D.s can also be slender. But her hypothetical test was a way of trying to measure the truth. If it could only be one or the other, she knew she would choose thinness without hesitation.

No one escapes. *Harper's* editor and essayist Sallie Tisdale recently wrote a poignant discussion of her own struggle. As with most of us, it began fairly early for her, and twisted her up pretty badly. Shrewdly, she pinpointed the symbol of the struggle—a number on a scale—and built her story around the getting and losing of that number, and all the nightmare suppositions and compensatory behaviors that came of it. At last she came to understand she could take it in one of two directions: as a struggle against the ideals of pop culture, or against herself.

Tisdale claimed in her essay that after many years, bit by bit, she was finally able to let it go. She allowed her body to find its balance and ease, accepting her form and appearance, her own spontaneous, healthful rhythms. I sent Tisdale's article to my friend who'd devised the doctorate-or-thinness riddle. My friend said she was glad for Tisdale, but could not imagine herself attaining the same enlightenment. She could not rid herself of the basic terror that completely letting go would lead to becoming a monster. I admired my friend's honesty, while getting more depressed than I'd dreamed possible, because I agreed with her. Even the smartest women contain this ticking grenade, this cluster of conditioned responses, always being re-sparked by images around us. No escape.

And the business of body size is only one snake on the Medusa-head of the tyranny, and the fear it has spawned—what writer Stephen Fried calls the beauty-industrial complex, pumping madly away. Gifted, soulful, artful women talk to one another, and too often the bottom line is still about the shelf-life of our sex appeal. Was it always, one wonders, this brutal, this skewed? "Freeing the last of the slaves," is how the late Orson Welles described the fledgling women's movement. Doubtless, Welles enjoyed the layers of inference available in that analogy, perhaps most particularly that freed slaves are at first as confused and unnerved as the newly stripped masters. Very often, the most comforting thing to do in years of uncertainty is to recreate little scale models of the old plantation.

Why do we agree to make ourselves over in the forms of prevailing currency? Because I think women finally most crave, and (ironically) will do nearly anything to achieve, an *Indian hold* in relationship. Bring your two arms to chest level before you. Grasp each forearm tightly with the other hand. With another person, that hold is unbreakable, unless you literally break arms. We look to be known and loved (and to give these things back) with that strength, and that parity. Corny, but there you have it. Something like what Yeats's narrator had in mind:

> *How many loved your moments of glad grace,*
> *And loved your beauty with love false or true;*
> *But one man loved the pilgrim soul in you,*
> *And loved the sorrows of your changing face.*

Finding this, living it, honoring it seems impossibly hard while each year every page and screen and billboard seem to scream a little louder: *Old, ugly, and no one to love.*

Reader, I can't fix it. I can hardly keep my wits in the midst of it. Yet I want to implore the beautiful young women with the world in their briefcases and terror in their hearts: *Stand against that terror. Stare it down.* Consider James Baldwin's wisdom: "The world's definitions are one thing, and the life one lives is quite another. One cannot allow oneself . . . to live according to the world's definitions: one must find a way, perpetually, to be stronger and better than that."

There may be no escape as we imagine it: no clean break, no sudden release, not even regression to pre-sexual innocence. Instead, we can trade increments of conscious choice, moment by moment, for increments of dignity, peace, and clarity. We know we will resist the marauding madness, the airbrushed pages reeking of chemical perfumes, the shrieking screens. I just wish we could step aside and let the tail-eating dragon roll past, over the horizon like a fiery wheel, swallowed for all time into the sea. But resistance means some degree of engagement, and that is ongoing, subtle, difficult business, a path strewn with live explosives, yes to this, no to that, a daily refiguring and renegotiation of all that filters in.

The older I get, the more I see this: If the continuum of possible responses to a cultural climate is a keyboard, the woman growing older improvises quiet variations on her theme. Every day the notation's amended, the chords subtly altered. She will pay this much attention, and no more. She will look after some details, let others fly. Above all, she tries to attend the small clear sound inside, like a struck tuning fork, that tells her what she really needs.

And yet I would be lying, to myself and to you, if I did not also tell you that even as this essay went into the world, my friends and I agreed: If we can afford it when the time comes, we might not be averse to getting, say, a facelift.

Make sense of it, if you dare.

Secret Formula

*J*OAN, I can see the end of my life.

This is what my friend David is telling me, over steaming primavera. He is looking at his plate, but he is not eating. David is turning forty, and he is mortified. I have known him several years, and for my money, his life is near-perfect. He wonders whether he and his partner shouldn't have a baby, to lengthen things out somehow. I lean forward.

David, I tell him. I saw this guy on the news the other night.

About a hundred years old, sitting in a worn armchair. Pet cockatiel hopping around on his shoulder. Lives in one of those old hotels downtown. Right—that's what I thought, too, at first: This is their Lite piece, the chaser for the dumpster-load of bad news. Codger with Heart of Gold. But then I notice the guy carries himself in some way that's different. He's tall, bony, and his voice quavers like it's underwater.

So the interviewing TV anchor is prompting him: What is this we hear about a formula for longevity? The camera pans around the old man's apartment and stops at his cubicle refrigerator, where the door swings open, revealing a lone bottle of *Lea & Perrins*, I swear it. Then the camera cuts back to the old man. His eyes are wide. He is telling the newsguy he's been taking two tablespoons of Worcestershire every day for the last, oh, fifty-sixty years. David, the old man is convinced it's kept him strong and healthy all this time.

Then he starts talking about how he used to hit all the glitzy night spots of this city, in its real heyday after the war, and he's remembering them all. Their names, the gossip, the craziness. He also remembers that in certain neighborhoods during a certain period, every single building was a whorehouse. But he is on local television, family channel, right? So he just says *house*—but with this *delicacy* that stops you cold. Every building was a *house*, he says, and his eyes get wide. He says the price often: *one dollar*. He says this on camera with shining eyes and a chalky voice, like an orphan remembering a feast. There is a beat. You can tell the interviewing newsman is choking there a moment, but then he pulls it together and presses on. I had been brushing my teeth—by this point I am standing in front of the television with my toothbrush in my hand.

As the old man reminisces, the TV station is flashing old black-and-white stills of places that are supposed to represent the kinds of places the old man knew. Women and men living it up in clubs and restaurants. High up in towers, busy thoroughfares, cliffs overlooking the sea. Each place looks like New Year's Eve. The women are a sort of meaty blur: Brunettes leaning along the bar, bobbed debutantes at tables, crisp linen, ice in glasses, deep cleavage. Lots of the women sit in somebody's lap, breaking up over a good joke. Your basic all-happy-hell breaking loose.

I forget about it until the next morning, after a typical night worrying about age and death and career and gossip. David, I worry about this man who walks his little girl to school every day over on Lake Street. Every morning he lets her get up on a concrete abutment next to the sidewalk, and every morning she makes her way along by grasping each metallic post along the abutment, pulling herself forward with each footstep, like pickets of a fence. Somehow, she never falls. The man walks so slowly alongside the little girl, patiently waiting and watching her. It drives me nuts. Will they be all right? Who will she become? What will they remember?

So I'm waking up that morning like any other, and I'm starting right up worrying about all the same stuff—and then I think of the old man. His smile was *guileless*, see? Faithful as a child's. I think of his voice, his papery skin, bright blinking eyes, nude of lashes like a turtle's. The few strands against the bald head, cobwebs.

David, I saw that someday I too will be so old that the only evidence of anything having happened to me that I *believe* happened to me, will be my word, and my word alone. And that word will be delivered in a voice watery with age, and kids and adults will look at me queasily, listening with that forced half-smile. They'll cock their heads; their eyes *might* fog up a second. Then they'll nod and turn away, maybe go brush their teeth, count themselves as broad-minded and generous to have affected the interest.

And then, I thought of the Worcestershire sauce.

Lying in bed some nameless workday morning, hearing that crazy dull yaaa of the city outside like a blank TV screen left on all night—my mind began flashing stills at me: The little bottle of *Lea & Perrins* standing at attention in the refrigerator, the old man's glistening eyes. And alone there in bed, in the stupid white noise of morning, for the first time in a very long time I felt my face working into an unfamiliar shape. And then I laughed.

As simple as that, David. I open my hands to him.

David is looking at me.

Do me this favor, I tell him. Whenever the Ingmar Bergman movie starts up in your head, think *Worcestershire sauce.* What do you think? Yes?

He looks for a long moment at me, like he's trying to decide something. Finally he shrugs, takes up his fork, and salutes me with it.

Better than a sharp stick, he offers, smiling kindly.

Our pasta is cold, but delicious.

The Alpha Male

SOMETHING about the way he came into D.'s apartment that night. Long, sure strides. Brisk and easy. Certain of his impact. The wind he generated blew along my cheek. I was talking to M., the violinist. Sprung from a long workweek, hair still drying from the workout, my arms loose and floaty, brain pleasantly softened by endorphins and champagne on an empty stomach. Glancing up at his cocky entrance, I caught his face a moment, glanced back to my friends, resumed talking with an eye on him.

He carried himself tall, though he wasn't. Graceful in his dense frame. Bit of a Nicolas Cage lookalike—must have known it—the requisite black everything: the leather jacket, the brown curly hair in a quasi-fifties sweep. Normally I laughed at this image, but—there was something about his face. I knew him from somewhere. When he approached, I stared at him and then it flooded back. "I know you. We met at D.'s last party. You were with the computers. We talked about your moving to the country after living in the city so long . . ." He shrugged. Maybe I'd embarrassed him. Maybe I was too ugly for him.

I was wearing a simple shirt and jeans and a down vest, my wet hair still pinned back on each side, which always made me look kind of sexless. I thought—the way women will, measuring ourselves against the acknowledged beauty model of the day and certain we fall hopelessly short of it by the end of a stupefyingly lonely night. I always think then of Laughton's Quasimodo— especially the final scene, when he murmurs to the heinous carved gargoyle beside him: "O, that I were made of stone, like thee."

I did remember this one from my composer friend's last party. He had been bored and restive, almost rude. All I'd sought then was polite chat. Social noise. He'd made it clear I didn't fit his agenda. Not on his dance card. *Tant pis*, little boy, I'd thought then, and wandered away. *Tant pis*, I thought now, and turned back to the others.

But he looked . . . different this time. I glimpsed him as he moved, so blatantly fond of himself, a touching caricature of suave control. Making just the right kinds of contact with the ga- thered crowd. Light on his feet, artful, shrewd, knowing just when to duck in and duck out. It was like watching ballet, or really good jump-rope. People looked into his face with frank admiration, and the women showed a bit of extra shine to their eyes.

Something in me made a tiny click as I watched him go. I got up, went into the bedroom full of coats. Shed the down vest, re- moved the hairpins and brushed out my drying hair. Then I went back. A little experiment. What the hell.

Men are amazing. I caught him sneaking glances at me. Each time I pulled my eyes away, and turned back to the others. But the young musicians were wearing on me. They were critical of the old ones, critical of the elders who continued to concertize even when they were old and (these young ones indicated) atrophied. They were haughty, these young ones, impatient to claim their own renown. They wanted their pathetic elders out of the way. "Why, Isaac Stern bought his own career," one young woman said. It made me feel rancid.

Then the Nicolas-type put on good dance music, music with a deep and sexy thrum that made you want to move. He moved a little to it. Across the room, I moved a little to it. Good music. I tried not to look at him moving so nice. I kept my face toward the people around me.

After a while the face began to ache from holding an interested expression toward the uncharitable noise of young musicians. I knew I had popped all the juice there was from these bright, tart berries. Another socially correct, useless evening: drag yourself to parties; follow the self-imposed mandate to Meet People; end up pondering Quasimodo. I made ready to leave and was making my way to bid my host goodbye. As I walked past him, Nicolas II said: Yo.

Yes?

Would you like to dance. He stood sort of sideways, looking sideways at me. I thought, Well. I didn't imagine it.

Yes. Sure. Wait. I ran away, brushed my hair again, heart thudding, came back, thinking: *don't think.*

Then I was moving with him in the darkened middle room, on a floor that was nice and rough-smooth like a real dance floor. We started to tell our lives. As he moved, he bragged about his career: his position, his talent, his power. Hilarious, yet his earnestness touched me. I told him the artists' colony had accepted me, but at that moment somehow it sounded obscure and puny, some bit of old lint in a camphor-soaked closet. Blinking only a moment to absorb and measure the possible import of this news, he pressed on: trips and cars and computers, foreign languages and prestige. Finally I decided to bite: Aren't you afraid of losing your soul, I asked.

Soul, no—heart, maybe, he said, as we walked deep into the dark backyard, beyond the back porch, and sat down on some old lawn furniture. It was the most amazing night. The wind blew cool, but not cold, and there was a quickening in it: one felt currents moving inside and outside. Vines hung long around us, and they smelled of deep, cool summer, and the soft fragrance hung there in the damp, dark yard, old roses and jasmine, even there in the middle of the city, and we both thought suddenly of Faulkner and the South. Had I read him, he asked. Long ago, I said, when I was too young to understand. Suddenly there was a breathlessness between us; I recognized it—everything would seem fulsome and important now, as if we needed to hold up a million little mirrors to each other, and agree, and agree, and agree.

The way he sat pleased me: open-lapped, elbows on thighs, hands open, shaping the air between his knees. He yammered on and on, of trying to transcend the high-powered corporate spin he commandeered. Of therapies and counseling. Of spirit and matter, of tantric yoga and tantric sex, of a cyber-punk future. It felt sweet and bold for me to listen with dancing eyes. He stretched harder with his bragging: Joyce and cummings and chakras, his college work: philosophy, logic, Japanese . . .

I wanted to laugh, but for some reason it all moved me. All of it. He was trying so hard. I put my chin in my hand and gazed at him in the windy, cool semi-dark and wanted him, and thought about what he'd be like. I kept pushing my hair back, letting my eyes dance but keeping the rest of my face grave and neutral, a full professor of the fragrant vines and the windy night.

Then he said something that faded my smile, something that gave back the rancid feeling. He said he believed he was an "alpha" male. A type who . . . had something extra. That he could take the lead anywhere, he said, any time he chose—if he chose—and that people would follow. I knew this was true as he said it, and loathed him for saying it. It was as if he'd told me he came from extreme royalty, but traveled incognito. Or that he had X-ray vision, or could fly or walk on water, but tried to use the gift responsibly. There I was: living evidence, a moth at the flame of his irresistible charisma, sitting rapt at his knees, having let something in me— that knew better—be eclipsed.

There is always that moment when you look at someone, and you realize how it could go either way. The vision shimmers in, and shimmers out. One moment they're a shining hothouse bloom of wit and warmth: the next they are a cold turd, an ugly absurdity. You can't decide. You want to get lost in their arms. You want to slap them away.

I felt angry, tired, and foolish. Tired of all the work of it. The chasm was too wide. I rose; snapped something like watch out for being subsumed by all those fancy toys. I wanted to fly away, dissolve—at very least to shut up my brain's dull monologue, the old man in the bathrobe who paces under a pale bulb in some stinking room, muttering an endless rosary of bitter imprecations. My own little *noir* Jiminy Crickett.

He followed me back in. We stood a stupid moment in the room where the coats lay. I gathered my things.

Suddenly he blurted: would you like to go dancing.

What? When, I said.

Right now, he said.

I glanced at the clock; it was 1 A.M. Maybe another time, I said.

Then I looked at him again in the dim light, at the attentive kindness in his face. Damn. When he offered to walk me to the car, I heard myself say yes, that I would like that; it was a rough neighborhood. I knew then that we would kiss, and my heart began to pound. As we walked, he started it all up again—the same boasting patter as in the dark yard, and again I felt weary. I tried to get back that first tender, amused feeling. How much *isn't that fascinating, aren't you just amazing* can anyone say? But as we got to the car, the wind blew hard, blew away all knowing better. It was a cold wind by then, and my heart raced with it. I leaned back against the car, searching his face, and after some more words at last he leaned toward me—just a brush of lips past lips—chaste, tentative. Stillness.

He stood back. I looked at him. We looked at each other and my eyes said, please, more. And he leaned again, and more. Soft, slow, and careful, feeling it out. Trying to see how we might fit. A little open, and my tongue moving to touch inside his mouth, a soft animal darting to touch a moment and be gone, and then more, and more, and we kept trying to find the ways that fit.

And then came that flooding surge of heat that makes a woman know she is meant to love men, an electrical flush from the chest to all extremities. My body seemed to be moving to its own choreography: pressing to him, breasts pushing against his chest, hands diving inside his jacket to circle his warm middle, pulling his hips to me, one hand moving up to cup the back of his neck, into his hair. It had been so long.

But there was no surge from him: instead, just a kind of steady, calm willingness. He tasted as fragrant as the summer air, as the Faulkner vines. The kisses were long, exploratory, informa-tion-gathering. I pressed into him: deep sweetness was there, but I had to work hard to get some. I was a hummingbird laboring at the nectar stem. I longed to see tenderness, to feel him surge. His gaze was steady. No surge. From time to time I put my lips to his neck, and sighed.

We looked at each other. He said, very softly, Do you want to be together tonight.

My chest tightened. Many gears whirred, and spun out a ticker-tape code. I was able at least to think this far, to read the internal telegram: not this night. But I wanted to kiss forever. I wanted to kiss until we floated into effortless, dreamy lovemaking on the bed of the cold night wind.

Let's wait, I said. It's more—tantric that way. Laughter.

I was sleepy and shivering. He began to rattle on some more, this time about his plans. He wanted to arrange an elite commune, to have his children by thirty-five . . .

Then something funny happened.

As he talked, a full-color Disney cartoon flamed up on a big screen just behind his head. I saw Sleeping Beauty there, this young man's life-mate, the brilliant goddess who would assume the throne alongside her prince one hallelujah day and bear his exquisite children. She had fairy-tale blond hair to her tiny waist, smiled beatifically, and moved among her admiring lessers like a kindly ballerina.

He was droning along: *And the really neat thing about robotics is when . . .*

I stood there smiling vacantly past his talking head, watching the film. I spotted myself in it, an elder handmaiden: one in a series. Pouring sherry at the princely pit stop. My job was to grace his training table, full-breasted, well-seasoned. Refine his technique for the real challenges, the true conquests before him. He would resume his journey refreshed, with clear conscience, good, noble, and true. A comic-book hero with well-muscled legs.

Alpha-Man.

I looked on.

I saw his life stretching before him as the sea does before a child—gleaming, vast. All the time in the world. And I was a colorful postcard tacked to his wallboard, a bit of something shiny, pretty souvenir of his worldliness.

I thought this: Born when I was in high school. A raw, red, wet, squawling thing when I was having regular menstrual periods. I could have birthed him.

I almost gasped aloud.

He waved as I ducked into my car. Blithe, serene. Pleased with his own equanimity. Reconfiguring his plans. I knew that I would never see him again.

And the kisses?

The kisses were a gift, I think. A gift from my fortieth summer, laughing as it waved goodbye in the cool night wind.

Her Proper Name

TO LIVE LONGER than one's mother lived to be feels like working a phantom limb.

As the year approaches, I imagine it will be like passing over a kind of equator: both viewer and what is viewed must change. One will see new country, I imagine, new colors—and in oneself, a new set of responses to that landscape. I must resist the sneaky superstition that the arbitrary date will claim me. That because of her there is a pre-prescribed limit to my time on earth; that I can go no further than she did, because of some imbedded cellular instruction. Because I came out of her.

My mother was forty-four when she died, my stepmother says. She says she saw the birthdate printed on my mother's driver's license. The license, encased in a thin red leather wallet, was among my mother's few last effects, kept by my father somewhere, unknown by us—like so much else—all this time.

I know the wallet. I know its blood-red color, exact color of my mother's lipstick. I know the wallet's thin, supple softness, its melting pliancy, its serious grown-up worn-leather smell, sharp, exciting the top of my nose even as I write. She pulled out the red wallet to pay for movies, for hamburgers, for groceries, for carousel rides in Encanto Park. We watched her waiting patiently at the edge of the swirling circle of swans, horses, tigers—and each time our swooping animals passed her, my little sister and I on parallel steeds, lushly muscled, frozen mid-lunge, glinting manes flying and nostrils flared, amid the throb and wheeze of Debussy's "Claire de Lune"—she smiled encouragingly, bravely, waved: then folded her arms back tightly across her chest again, hunched as if against cold, though days were warm in Encanto Park. Dark sunglasses blotted her identity so that she appeared almost invisible, a weakly smiling cipher, all red lipstick and sunglasses, short black curls pushed behind her ears, shoulders hunched in the shade of the turning carousel. Always bundled in big plaid flannel shirts and baggy black trousers. Hair cropped short and shapeless, mouth set in a stoic line. Peeping from below the flapping trousers, canvas wedgie sandals with white cotton socks. Her feet so small.

As I grew up I stared with interest at those feet. Her toes were deformed, gnarled under, permanently squashed into the shape of a pointy shoe, great defending knobs at the joints of the big and little toes, where the feet made their brave stand against the punishing shoes. I watched her dressing at the doorway of the dark closet in my parents' bedroom—wondered at her pear-like breasts, mysterious pale buttocks that seemed cool and flaccid, mysterious triangle of dark hair at her crotch. When we undressed at the Jewish community center, all the other grown women in the locker room looked that way too, and I watched them, mesmerized, appalled. The women turned away and bent over their clothing busily to show less of themselves; moving quickly, as if to conceal what they knew was grotesque. Why did women look this way? Ripply and mushy and pale, with strange pendulous things, and hair where I had none. Was this how I had to grow up to look?

Momma! Look at me! Momma, watch! We feed the ducks, running backwards, laughing with fear as they squawk and screech and stick their necks out long, snapping and honking, advancing greedily on our sacks of crumbled bread. How we love the tired green willows trailing in olive-colored waterways; how we love the green algae smell of the turgid water! We plead to paddle the paddleboat, we plead to have just one more ride, we plead for an ice cream, for popcorn, for Cokes, and she relents, and relents, and pays and pays from the blood-red, leathery-smelling wallet for our ice cream, our popcorn, our bread to feed the ducks. She indulged us our vision of a physical world sopped with magic: Long flights of concrete steps in downtown Phoenix fronting the post office, the bank, the courthouse—Mayan ruins or Egyptian pyramids, begging to be scaled. *Encanto Park, Sky Harbor Airport, Cinema Park Drive-In:* monolithic thrills, sheathed with promise. My chest still pinches at the sounds of the words.

I don't need to ask to see the driver's license photo again. I know the photo. It is worse than disturbing, or sad: it is frightening. Anyone who looked at the picture could have known. Should have known. Should have taken one look and known. She stands for the photo as if before a firing squad, staring fixedly at the camera, a prisoner being booked; expressionless, not resisting, not present. A mug shot. Her face is drawn, pallid; she looks straight ahead into nothing. Tendons stand out in her neck, so rigidly does she hold her jaw. Her mouth—that mouth, whose last message of sagging corners will always be with me—is set in a single, taut line. Determined to cleave to the rules of the apparent world, she stands for her driver's license photo to be snapped. *Momma. Please wake up Momma.*

She weighed perhaps a hundred pounds. Dark-eyed, dark-lashed, perfectly proportioned and curvaceous within her scant five feet. In early photos she wore her shining black hair swept up, or bobbed shoulder-length with bangs, the modes of the day. Later she would wear it cropped and permed, like Deborah Kerr's in *King Solomon's Mines*. Black hair against creamy skin, deep red lipstick; wine-veering-to-blood. Wide-spaced almond eyes, long, silky lashes. We gaped in awe at our pretty mother. She smelled of Arpège. Her skin seemed velvety-moist, luminous like a lily lit from inside, wafting the faint scent of cold cream. Always, my mother wore an expression of dreamy mourning. Her features were delicate, symmetrical, her eyes wistfulness itself, and there was the faintest downturn to the edges of her mouth—a terrible secret hinted at those falling corners.

My father would say after her death that the strongest element in his courtship of Marion was pity. They were both secretaries in the second world war. Her feet had bothered her; he had massaged them. Look at the photos: There is the strapping man, like a magazine ad for New York City, striding the sidewalk with zest and clarity, big limbs swinging easily in the loose-cut, heavy suit, folded *Times* clasped in one large capable hand, headful of thick waving hair, dark eyes alert and purposeful. There, in the other picture, is the tiny woman: eyes lifted bashfully to the intruding camera as if found out. Halter top and shorts, fine hair brushing her shoulderes—a Hellenic statue come to life, shy of intruding mortals.

As a girl she was precocious and articulate, if agonizingly shy. I believe my mother wore long braids then. She wore middy blouses to school, the sailor-style for girls, with an oversized bow tied at the chest—perhaps over pleated skirts. Well read, bright, she had skipped a grade in school. She loved and knew music, dance, art, literature, movies. New York must have been the bar-none haven for young people of the '30s and '40s—the concerts, the park, the films, food, museums. The New York Public Library.

And the subway. One family friend who knew them, and who claims to be a bit telepathic, "sees" my youthful parents, she tells me, on the subway in the early days of their courtship. I remember my father being drawn to an old Ernest Borgnine film called *Marty*. In it, an awkward, blue-collar worker courts a painfully shy young woman in New York. There was something queasy and compelling about their hesitant romance, set against the backdrop of the city—its subway, where the young lovers met and parted amid clammer and clang, added poignancy to their courtship, to the innocent folly of human striving. The couple's fumbling sexuality confused and troubled me as a child. I believe those elements drew my father to the film, reminding him of his earnest young self, courting the young Marion.

Perhaps, at the beginning, my mother's soft melancholy seduced my father. Perhaps her sad other-worldliness piqued his curiosity and begged protection. He must have felt manly and tender beside her, a sentry to her delicacy. But my mother could not have laid plans to snare my father, in the calculating manner women are sometimes chided for. She was too genuinely mired in her own sad dreams to feign anything. The shadows across her features, even as a very young beauty, were already so deeply part of her, for whatever reasons, that from the earliest photos she looked far distant: poised to vanish.

I have memorized every photo. She looks almost translucent in them, a pearly ghost, even as a girl. Even as a beautiful young woman, my mother looks as though her dearest wish is to just be allowed to fade away—barely registering in the light of the living world. Yet her womanly shape and bearing speak of earthly appetites, and when she smiles it is brilliant—pretty lips wide in glad abandon, dazzling teeth. There must have been a time when

71

she dreamed of many men, and then of my father, with secret, half-formed wishes.

She came from a large, overbearing mother in the classic mold—the terrifying Bertha. I can imagine the jokes my father must have made. Like any of so many aging matrons one saw patrolling the boardwalks with their ice creams at Miami Beach: zeppelin breasts blooping over thick midsections; squinting and clucking, nasal whine of complaints and gossip rising and dimming like plaintive insect-drone in the humid day; strolling and tanning big bodies on the beaches and boardwalk—acres of white dimpling flesh, blue-red in the harsh light.

Bertha visited once. We drove with our mother to fetch her at Sky Harbor Airport. Instantly I feared her. Once she'd settled her bulk into the seat beside my mother in the car, she began to recite to my mother bad news and malicious gossip in that sour, deprecating nasal saw. It made me want, even as a very small child, to run away. My sister and I rode in the backseat. I remember my mother's grim posture. I watched the back of her head from the backseat of the turquoise '49 Ford as we drove home. Her head was stiff, fixed toward the horizon: She was driving as if at gunpoint.

My mother's father was named Bernard; this much was passed on, but little else. He was dead by the time we met Bertha. I've seen only one photo of him: scowling into the camera, dressed in a baggy suit, posing on the descending steps of a traincar in a New York station. No other details of him have filtered down, and in my vain and self-absorbed growing up I never asked my father about him (as with so terribly much else), and now it is too late. But the photo, and Bertha's manner, suggest why young Marion may have suffered so. She must have grown up a prisoner of others' anger.

My mother's life must have seemed a bad dream to her from

the start, relieved occasionally by the things she loved, mild interludes. A series of brown-gold sepia photos shows her posing beside fountain-pools with ducks sailing on them, in a park. She is wearing a sun hat, smiling shyly into the camera against the late afternoon light; light glints in floating sepia stars off the fountain-pool water. She sits at the edge of the pool with her eyes closed in the sun, resting—as if, already, so tired—in classic cameo profile, hair swept up, neck arcing into delicate chin and cheekbones. The words "Saratoga Springs" are inscribed on the back of the photos, in a graceful hand I do not recognize.

When as a girl I asked my mother about her childhood, she told me, in her soothingly musical voice, about the middy blouses. She said she loved homemade blackberry jam on fresh bread. She loved the song "To a Wild Rose," by Edward MacDowell. I learned to play a simple version of the song for her on the old upright piano she'd bought for my practice, and I too came to love its pensive, tender theme. The song became my mother to me, over years.

My stepmother says my mother was briefly married to another man before she married my father, and that the marriage had been annulled. Marion must have been desperate to get away, to seize any chance to leave, and in those days, marriage was the sanctioned chance. Did the annulled marriage make her sad? Ashamed? Was the sex awful for her? What did my mother long for? What words formed her thoughts? Would she have liked the woman I became, with my rough language, my haste and impetuousness, my careless unmended clothing and spartan apartment, my perennial bachelorhood?

I think not. I think she'd have been dismayed, maybe even wounded by her oldest daughter's sheer garishness. She loved what was demure, what was classically feminine, gracious. I pleased her less and less as I grew—I answered back, had my own ideas, but worst, I was ashamed of her.

73

I was in the grip of dawning adolescence, desperate to be like the images I saw in magazines and on television, longing for shining linoleum and modern gadgetry, pining to live as people did in commercials for refrigerator-freezers and fingernail polish. But it was more than that. I was ashamed of our shabby house, its worn furniture and odd, mismatched plastic plates and cups, ashamed of my mother's baggy clothes and no-longer-tended hair, because—I now believe—I was confused and frightened. I believe I sensed in some deep, inchoate way that these various evidences signaled far more than simple carelessness.

I was eleven when she died. We could not wake her one morning. My father called it a heart attack in her sleep. The truth is still unclear. It took me twenty years to consciously acknowledge that suicide can be a cumulative thing, with actual death quietly slipping in at some moment of least resistance. A coroner's report described an excess in her system of barbiturates that had been prescribed for my father, who was easily twice her size. To quote again the family friend: "It is possible your mother just wanted some sleep."

We moved away then, to another state and city, and for the remainder of my father's life we almost never spoke of her, nor of the manner of her death. (No one felt a need to comment when my father and stepmother began volunteering time on suicide prevention hotlines in our adopted city.) We still cannot name her. We cannot say Mom, or Mother, even from this distance in time, my sister and I. We say Our Mother. Do you remember when Our Mom. Because to utter the word as a proper name, Mother, or Momma, still makes us flinch—we are stricken with inexplicable queasiness. It is not pain, but a queer abashedness. I suppose you could call it shame. But it is something else, too: a dull, quasi-sensation, like touching a very old scar, or stirrings in a phantom limb.

If I could, I would try to explain to Marion now that I became a good woman. That I do good work, have loving friends. That little sister made a family, three fine sons! That we cherish the childhood our mother gave us.

I would try to make her know what it meant, then as now, to be allowed to hurl ourselves shrieking, fully dressed, into the Pacific Ocean at Santa Monica, the first time children of the desert had ever laid eyes upon an ocean. Or the birthday she went to great trouble to find my birthstone, a simple opal on a delicate chain, describing her journey to find it as if it had been a mystical quest. I have clear and grateful flashbacks of ballet lessons, library trips bearing towers of books, movies, hamburgers and malts, special little gimcracks she'd hunted down for us, stories she told as we went bumping along in the old Ford on unpaved desert roads (a witch lived under the nastiest stretches). My father, a charismatic and hard-drinking professor, was rarely with us, and so we three became an odd team by default: tiny sad woman, two wildly vital little girls. I would explain I had wanted to help her not be sad, but that little girls at eleven and nine cannot yet name, let alone help, that kind of sadness. One day, maddened and crushed by my father's relentless, reckless straying, by her loneliness in a conservative southwest town so barren and remote from her beloved New York, by an era which turned its back on bereft women—women whose psychic and physical surivival was so utterly dependent on marriages to inaccessible husbands that those husbands actually pitied their wives too much to leave them—she succumbed.

I am convinced she didn't mean to abandon us. She simply lost whatever was left that had kept her with us. Yes, she was a chronic melancholic, but just a few years later, there might have been help for that, a chance for it to play out differently. A few years later we have crisis lines, support groups, networks, therapists, shelters. In her time and place, the word "divorce" was uttered with the same hushed horror as the word "abortion." In that day there was great, shameful stigma attached to any hint of even having sought counseling—much better to hide the black eye, the crushed heart. Here is how that family friend describes the lot of women then: "You just injected your grapefruit with vodka and shut up." And what help may have existed cost money; money came from husbands. In short, no way out. No recourse—at least not to one so purely and comprehensively exhausted, one who believed herself so hopelessly, irrevocably isolated. As if hanging from a high ledge by fingertips, her grip finally, simply, gave.

I will make her life known. I will honor her this way. And in this year of passing that invisible equator, my invisible scars will stir again. Thereafter, it's uncharted country.

Lots More Pencils, Lots More Books

S O I WENT back to college last summer. No kidding. See, I'd
been an early dropout. Ran away and joined the Peace
Corps—because I wanted to *Live*. You know how it goes. Whatever the parents are or were, the kid is honor-bound to puncture
any expectations that she or he might actually follow suit. Hell,
that is the *task* of kids born into post-mid-century or so—or maybe
it is the province of most kids most of the time: striking out to seek
one's fortune, against prevailing pressures to be butcher, baker,
mover and shaker. It's queer to have lived long enough to notice
the pendulum swing back and forth across a generation or two:
My most wildly iconoclastic friends seem *mandated* to bear
children who will become born-again fundamentalists, or join the
Marines. And then *their* kids will move into communes, quoting
Whitman and so on. Anyhow, in my case, the trajectory was clear:
If Papa was a college teacher, distinguished and beloved in the
academy, fine: You fled the academy—*until* you'd lived and

worked long enough in the world to begin to see where it might be real helpful to understand a few things better. Like sex, and labor unions, and Chekhov, and Bosnia. Well, like Chekhov.

The Master of Fine Arts program turned out to be a sort of combination boot camp/prep school for grownups. I wonder how anyone who has not been in school awhile can ever be ready for the level of discourse following a lecture or class that—ah—rather distinctly signals we're not in Kansas anymore. Conversations took off like a greyhound-race at the starting gun; people peppered their talk with references to every big-deal poet or writer the world had ever saluted. Words like "monolithic" and "verisimilitude" kept popping up. They were *walking sets of great books*, these students. But the best thing was, they ranged in age from mid-twenties to late fifties (many of them teachers in their breadwinning lives). They had lived in the world a while, therefore brought to their studies a kind of passion that the lately hatched might have trouble comprehending. A professor told a friend of mine that forty-year-old women made the best students on earth, and I don't doubt that now. Just scanning my reading list—titles I had longed all those years to catch up with—brought tears to my eyes. *Glad I lived this long*, was all I could think, snuffling.

But all that great earnestness—nonstop, dawn past dark, with scarcely time to pee—made some seventy faculty and students dazed, and disoriented. What month was this again? What city? So when it came time for the final dance, held in a darkened barn with a table full of cheap wine and a pounding sound system, we fell forward into it like grateful androids come for repair. There we moved to a mishmash of begged and borrowed music—King Sunny Ade, Prince, Talking Heads, the Supremes, Ruben Blades, Marvin Gaye. I looked over and saw the fiction teacher who had earlier been intoning that our annotations may be returned to us, annotated—this guy was doing something that looked like epileptic hopscotch, with another fiction teacher who had carried herself at a cool distance during the residency, her smile cryptic and veiling as a painted fan. She was strutting and striding around him, elbows working, an emissary from the Ministry of Silly Walks. Teachers boogied with students; students with teachers— not a breath of sexual hijinx, of course, because everybody had been strictly warned against the disastrous consequences of crossbreeding. In fact one alumnus had ruefully tagged the place "a hotbed of chastity." Alas, it was just simpler that way.

Yet here before me, in this writhing brainpool, was good faith. Here was vitality. The dancing poets and writers were hope substantiated; committed, savvy, hugely alive—not bad to look at, either. I was standing by the wine table, guzzling icewater and admiring the sweaty scene, when a young program assistant wandered up. He was perhaps a college senior, working for the graduate program during the summer; he'd driven me in from the airport when I'd arrived, and we'd had a pleasant chat. "Hey, John," I clapped him on the back, genuinely happy to see him. "Last day! Great time, eh? Great program." I gestured at the rippling crowd, the handsome MFA candidates and their advisors, accomplished novelists and poets with reputable bodies of work for sale that very minute at fine bookstores everywhere—working it all out on the wooden barn floor. "Remarkable, yes?"

He nodded. "Yeah," he said, rubbing his chin thoughtfully as he surveyed what I was pointing to. There was a pause. "It's always good to see older folks having fun."

My eyes must have lost focus a few minutes, and I remember little else of that night—except that for a while, I simply couldn't believe I'd lived that long: long enough to hear a comment which kindly and cheerfully shunted me to the Marginalia section. Am I still glad I lived this long? Well: Somebody's got to account for it, don't they. And even if it's by default, we're that standard's bearers now.

Pass the Chekhov, please.

Never Safe

OW DO I tell how it is about myself and movies? First I test people with the opening line: *I cannot go to movies that I know will hurt.* Here I wait to see if an eyebrow floats up, even the littlest bit. If the eyebrows stay level, if the eyes underneath do not gleam with superior irony, I continue: Once the image goes in, I explain, it will never come out.

Take the first movie I ever saw, *Twenty Thousand Leagues Under the Sea.* For a long time afterward I lived in terror of a giant squid squirting black ink, gripping hapless sailors in oily tentacles. I kept seeing the sinister green eye of the submarine *Nautilus* pushing fast through the surface of the ocean, as demented James Mason hurled his own sub full-throttle into his enemies' ships. What would happen to handsome Kirk Douglas, trapped on the *Nautilus,* battling the squid in his striped sailor shirt? Everything augured; everything *loomed.*

The trauma to my little mind was not so much about blood and gore. It was more about the impalement of humans on the sharp spear of evil, their maddeningly unjust suffering. At five or six, I found sitting in the darkened movie theater to be like flailing in a night storm at sea. Immense images and roaring sound crashed over me like waves as I thrashed for breath. I learned early to stumble over intervening legs, purses, and popcorn and make for the lobby (blessedly well lit), to dawdle in the bathroom, to stare at the colored boxes in the candy counter. When my heartbeat had finally calmed, I'd peek back at the screen through the chink in the swinging upholstered lobby doors. I could control the terror that way.

But it never got easier. After *Leagues* came *The Wizard of Oz*, which left me so dreading the specter of a twisting black tornado on the horizon that I pleaded with my parents to buy a house with a storm cellar (we lived in Arizona). Disney did me no favors, what with *Pinnochio, Bambi, Snow White,* and *Sleeping Beauty.* Nor, as I grew, did any Broadway-based musical. After each I dabbed at swollen red eyes and began to seek out men who looked like Rossano Brazzi or Gordon McRae. After spending Saturday afternoons with epics such as *The Ten Commandments* or *Ben Hur,* I was convinced, despite being raised a liberal Unitarian, of a shrewd and harsh father-God who waited a little too long before rescuing His own. And what about the Red Sea closing over Pharaoh's innocent horses: Did they deserve to drown?

It's as if my heart took in the drops that ophthalmologists use to dilate pupils. My heart is permanently dilated. *The Diary of Anne Frank* drilled the pitiless eee-aww of Nazi sirens into memory's ear, shaking me to this day. *Alfie* and *Ship of Fools* laid open smoldering sexual tensions and inequities I had no names for yet—knotted, dark, unresolvable. *Judgment at Nuremburg, West Side Story*—ordeals. With *Elmer Gantry, Butterfield 8, Hud,* and *The L-Shaped Room,* adult desire and wretchedness seeped into me like an invisible virus, infecting my dreams as I tossed back Raisinets and cherry Cokes. My mother, a delicate, lonely woman who pined for her native New York, often sat beside me in the air-conditioned dark. Faced with row upon row of empty days in a dusty Arizona town, she depended on movies to help fill the vast, blank screen of her life in the raw, 1950s Southwest.

I am certain that my sad, tiny mother thought she was educating me well, rooting me in rich cultural soil out there in the desert, nourishing me on Cinerama sophistication. In many ways, of course, she was. But how could she guess that her little daughter's mind was itself raw film? That everything seen through the lenses of these eyes would play and replay in the impressionable brain behind them? Going to movies won't always be this hard, I'd tell myself as a girl, but it's still that hard. Fast-forward with me through *Psycho,* and a lifetime of racing away up carpeted aisles, peeking back through the chinks in lobby doors.

The only thing being grown up has done is to teach me to plan for the disability. I learn every detail of what to expect from a film, questioning people, weighing and sifting opinions. I scan every review and study advance publicity (the stills for *Alien* told a lot). Like anyone, I love to be moved, to laugh, to learn, and of course to escape into movies. But because of this dilated heart condition, I can allow my eyes to remain open only when I have reason to believe that a film will be not only good, but safe.

This means no sadism. No psycho-horror. No relentless jackhammering of the senses. Little manages to survive this fine-mesh screen. European ensemble work—*May Fools, Dark Eyes*—does well, as do offbeat sleepers: *When Father Was Away on Business.* But even this strategy can backfire. Films that most of the world considers harmless as an after-dinner mint can grind me into granules. Add a heart-slicing music score like Ennio Moricone's to the haunting theme of childhood loss, as in *My Life as a Dog* or *Cinema Paradiso,* and you're asking for a face that will look bee-stung beyond recognition for three straight days.

Sometimes, despite every precaution, I find myself blinking before a moving picture nearly certain to imprint nightmares— queasy-making stuff that will run and rerun in my mind's nonstop projection booth. And I know I will have to decide once again, amid all those enviably mild and self-possessed people in that dark theater, whether to stay and risk opening a new file of horror, or to play it safe and run away. Maybe this is just plain silly; maybe it's pure neurosis. I wonder. Some people can calmly seat themselves in the frontmost car of a roller coaster, holding their arms high during the most sickening plunge, while others can't. Some people can walk out of *Silence of the Lambs* and resume their lives. I wonder if these distinctions aren't finally just some genetic predisposition, like the attached ear lobe.

That's it. An extra gene, for the dilated heart.

Getting It Back

SITTING in traffic hating everything—the cold fog, angry car horns, prickling nerves, my numb rear end; the sullen, blank faces mirroring my own—I spot a little girl in leotards walking along the sidewalk, led by her mother. The girl has on black ballet slippers and a diaphanous white nylon-net tutu. She walks with studied care, as if she carries the seeds of all art and magic within her small body.

I know that walk. My own diaphanous costume was turquoise, with turquoise sequins, when I was an angel in Pearl Daily's Ballet School production of *Hansel & Gretel*, in Sunnyslope, Arizona. My scene was where the angels swoop in from heaven and do a little dance around the sleeping children. Every note of the famous theme, by Humperdinck, is imprinted in memory, as well as the lyrics affixed to that theme, a version of the "Now I Lay Me Down to Sleep" prayer. Fourteen angels watch do keep: Two to whom 'tis given . . . to guide my way to heaven.

Rehearsals were during the afternoons. My heart must have

nearly stopped when it came time for the actual performance, which was given in the evening, before a makeshift grandstand of viewers, among whom sat my mother and my father, in an outdoor courtyard smelling of orange blossoms. If ballet class had been heaven—with its hardwood floors flooded with sunlight, its barres and mirrors and upright piano, its cluster of very young children milling and fluttering in their leotards like a convention of baby blackbirds—then dancing at a formal performance outdoors, at night, in turquoise sequins before a smiling audience, was as good as sitting in God's right hand.

In those days the universe was so literally sopped with magic your shoes nearly squished in it as you walked. The quality of light and air in 1950s Phoenix helped: Perspective loomed, aromas ran riot, colors splashed and seeped. Stars and moon arced over a familiar and mysterious diorama of rain-smelling desert and malt-smelling drugstores, of comic books, municipal swimming pools, lightning, saguaro and mesquite, horny toads. The fizzing salvo of cola bubbles under the nose was enough to make you delirious. Now I have to drink a lot of black coffee to get anything approaching that level of breathlessness—and of course, even wired to the eyeballs, or giddy on champagne, it's not the same.

Here is the trick we are called on again to reinvent in adult life: Transcending what a friend calls the heroic monotony. We do what we must and fall asleep at the wheel. Routine inures us, habit and duty make us cranky and dull. No matter how often our teeth vibrate after reading the tragic headline or even after dodging our own terrifying close call, we soon slide back into numbness and to a strange waterlevel of discontent.

Novelist Edna O'Brien has noted "loneliness, physical and metaphysical, stamped on every face I see." To me, it looks more as though people stuck in traffic or grocery checkout lines are simply waiting in line to die. Sometimes I fancy that we now pay therapists the way an earlier generation bought brushes or Bibles or pep tonic from traveling salesmen: We are hungry for the contact; for purpose, faith, and possibility. I believe that you can remember possibility, that you can make yourself see and feel with something like the hair-raising X-ray vision of childhood but that you have to work at it in odd ways to get back even a shiver—to be mesmerized again by motes of dust floating through a light shaft, by the blind pink earthworms writhing in the street after a rain. You must recognize the triggering object or image and let it draw from some invisible recess, as a wick does oil, the wash of wonder—still living in our cells somewhere, like genetic memory. But it does fade quickly, and you must be ready for the sadness that inevitably follows.

Perhaps we should all keep a dashboard shrine or carry in our pockets the objects that remind us of the spirit of our very young self, the dream that once took us far, the uncorrupted soul. Imagine: Once we thought certain items so numinous it was only logical and reasonable to assume we could make wishes on them.

I took inventory of mine yesterday. Two clearie marbles, one Egyptian blue, one robin's egg blue. The cap of a eucalyptus acorn, still very pungent. An art-deco pendant in the shape of a trident, studded with fake rubies. A kazoo. A dented Mexican jumping bean. A tarnished cameo charm in the shape of a young girl's ponytailed head. A delicate painted-fan earring. An old Double Bubble Gum Fortune ("Don't fear change. It's for the best"). Carved ornate chopsticks of polished dark wood. A pink seashell, a purple amethyst. And a photograph. The photo is of my infant face, open and fresh as a sunrise. I keep it propped by my desk—not for vanity but for whatever subliminal cues my heart can read there of that first nature, that way of seeing. I have to be reminded every day.

A friend found me this quote, by memoirist Lucy Grealy: "I

once thought that when you understood something, it was with you forever. I know now that this isn't so, that most truths are inherently unretainable, that we have to work hard all of our lives to remember the most basic things."

Maybe it would be impossible to function all the time with too wide a lens, as an adult. Too much to sustain, and still move forward on the sidewalk, still wind the clock at night with resolve. Maybe that's why artists have tough lives and sometimes go mad.

But I would wager it is better than waiting in line to die.

When It is Good

MY EDITOR TWIRLED her wineglass across the table from me, looking thoughtful. "I want you to write about when it is good," she said finally. "When you actually enjoy being alone." No doubt she guessed this might prove a real stretch.

The truth is, there is plenty that is good about it. More than what is bad—though that belief shifts and ripples daily, along with the private states of things. Still, in my mind's gallery, the glad-I-lived-this-long hall of fame, some of the loveliest memories have had everything to do with being alone. In each, the humblest particulars stand out like tiny jewels.

There was an evening: sitting at the word processor, cup of tea in hand, Catalan guitar on the FM, wearing my favorite old flannel shirt, a beat-to-hell pink-and-gray-checked affair that feels buttery as a baby blanket. A settled stillness from the dark streets enfolded my little apartment. I looked around, blinked and suddenly felt a dawning.

I was happy.

It lasted long enough for me to breathe it, to silently name its elements like beads on a rosary: The people I loved were safe and well. I was safe and well. I had work before me I loved, and no one would forbid me to pursue it. I was not in unmanageable debt. I had peace, autonomy, creative freedom. I may not have had a mate or children there with me. But I had beloved friends and family, including children, who cared very much about me, counted on seeing me, and wouldn't hesitate to help if I needed it.

Isn't this something like what people have founded nations and died in wars for?

Other scenes filter in, so common that citing them makes me sound like the reformed Ebenezer Scrooge on Christmas morning: streets of my city, brilliant with moving life. The Sierra Nevada looming like great gentle snow-covered dinosaurs alongside my car. Music, art, sunlight, air. All of it goes in. All of it counts.

For a writer, to be able to kick around alone for long periods is as vital as breathing. In my case, much of that time is spent very simply: running in the park, swimming, reading, walking, driving, catching a movie. I admit a certain sadness about the enforced isolation, but there is also serenity. At these intervals, thinking wanders free, idiosyncratic and random as it likes. Only then can a certain interiority be accessed, a chance to shuffle the complex data with the mundane, to register gathered notions and impressions, to view my own incongruous presence in the grid of lives around me: to muse on the miracle of musing.

One can't easily think like this in any kind of company, whether it's the water-heater repairman, the nine-year-old nephew, or the friend you meet for tea. For it works a separate musculature to address others, to anticipate needs and frame responses, to stay in the volleying. A soft internal monologue hums during daily interchange, giving cues and tips and cutoff signals like the earplug murmuring in a news anchor's ear. Taken away from that, a deeper monologue drifts up. Some of it is gibberish, but some of it has weight, like glints of gold in a sifting pan. In solitude I slowly come to know one from the other.

There is a Möbius-strip quality to the riddle of aloneness: I both crave it and dread it. To lose it is to remember why I chose it. Travel, house guests, even a lover come to roost awhile—all reacquaint me in a hurry with the reasons I keep a solitary style. So seldom in the business or homemaking day does anyone get time alone to breathe, to rest, to organize thought, to take a longer view. As soon as regular blocs of it are even temporarily postponed, my instinct, strong as a swimmer's groping to the surface for air, is to strive madly to get it back. Otherwise, some basic equilibrium is lost, a well-being, an awareness that focuses the rest of existence. I can't easily know you, unless I can frequently be allowed to remember, alone, who I am.

And yet too much can be frightening. The haunting danger, for a woman living alone, is of growing brittle with habit, closing off to spontaneity, sliding into an almost feral wariness. Self-pity's the worst enemy of all, and I now see, an unaffordable luxury. When I was younger—read, immortal—it had a certain romantic cachet. As kids we thought it pretty to sulk and languish, leering smokily at the world from behind our own potential. Later we find nobody's looking, and anyway there's no time for it. For years I kept a cartoon sent by a friend, showing a small sign posted at the edge of a large body of water: *Sea of Self-Pity: No Wallowing.*

Like an astronaut's disorientation after a long time in orbit, perspective can warp in unrelieved solitude. You need some form of cold water to smack you awake—to keep paranoia at bay, to avoid lapsing into viewing your own aloneness as a kind of tragic freefall. Conversation, fresh air, a change of scene—whatever it takes, you must build in antidotes—must regenerate daily your own grid of meaning: your own reasons to live. It is not that this existential bottom-line is not ultimately true for everyone else. It is that the loner has less to distract her from it.

I notice that people who do not spend much time alone have trouble understanding the struggle against the specter of loneliness. It's tough to convey, because the words have become transparent from overuse. Far as we imagine we've come as a society, the woman alone is still viewed with a certain unease: Why isn't she with someone? If that woman stays observant, and compassionate, she feels less and less that prickle of indictment and more and more the larger, kinder understanding that all arrangements are finally provisional. Lovers, marriages, families, careers— all turn out to have limited shelf-lives; at very least, never what they seem. It's a revelation, and a comfort. We begin to let go of a frenzy for permanence, a belief that grace is final, granted by some ineffable Other. It's no longer a binary world. Things come and go.

But we are never so detached as to be immune to longing. Composer Marvin Hamlisch once described returning to his apartment after a glittery evening of winning several Oscars for his music. Puffed with glory as he walked to his door, he suddenly wilted upon opening it. He'd just won three Oscars, been hailed and adored—and then he was gazing at his unchanged apartment, empty and dark and silent, realizing that the cat litter needed changing. What did the fame and fortune matter, if there were not something deeper, warmer, more abiding and palpable than a roomful of trophies, awaiting him where it counted?

A shrewd friend of mine, who is not American, snorts with impatience at this plaintive little parable. "Why do Americans always imagine it should ever be any other way? We all have to face the same mundanenesses, the same terrors. We're all born alone, we're all going to die alone someday. It is the cat litter which is transcendent, not the Oscars!"

I have to laugh. My friend's point echoes the familiar Zen adage, "Before satori, chop wood and carry water; after satori, chop wood and carry water." And this vision—of being both humbled and exalted in simple acts of daily attention; of being profoundly moved by the passionate persistence of the life in and around us—brings me squarely back to the mysterious joy of living quietly alone. The late Raymond Carver wrote:

> *And did you get what*
> *you wanted, from this life, even so?*
> *I did.*
> *And what did you want?*
> *To call myself beloved, to feel myself beloved on the earth.*

The music of streets and seasons, an old flannel shirt: the woman alone finds her belovedness in unexpected ways.

Female Trouble

*G*ENTLEMEN, turn the page.

What follows is not for the squeamish. I promise I've only your well-being in mind when I suggest you go do other things for a while. Write a book, shoot a few baskets, play an instrument, entertain a child, cook up something divine. I'm an equal opportunity segregationist today.

For I'm talking to the women now. This is a dispatch from the field. The field is called A Certain Age, and the battle, as best I understand it, is with our own hormones. It may be PMS, it may be perimenopause—the broaching edge of menopause. The enemy is invisible, but its weapons are real. And it's gaining on us.

Like a character in an old Vincent Price movie, tormented by a split-identity whose evil side is taking over, I want to offer my impressions before it is too late—rather like the last testament of the poor guy who is so rapidly turning into *The Fly* he will soon be able only to buzz. It's better to talk about early in the cycle, while calm and coherent. Women will know at once what this means.

The first eight to ten days of the menstrual cycle is often the only time when many of us feel, act, and look normal.

Ah, those precious days. My body is familiar, sturdy, reliable, going about its duties with cheer and brio. Belly is flat, legs look like legs, breasts fit the bra. Hooks hook, buttons button. My complexion's clear; my conversation logical; I am capable of basic social graces and paying my bills. I make hopeful plans, sleep at night, waken with interest in the day before me; eat sensibly, enjoying the cup of coffee or glass of wine. Existence makes sense, the universe has order, even joy.

Got it? That's eight, with luck maybe ten, days of every month's thirty or so. Sometimes, normalcy barely lasts a week.

The rest of each month? In a word, hell.

To document these cyclical werewolfian breakdowns, I began taking notes in one of those big month-at-a-glance calendars. The results were pretty sad. Like a giant jigsaw puzzle, last year reveals the larger mosaic: Repeated, systematic ruination of a helpless, innocent woman. Right there on paper: Female trouble.

Its phases are so specific women can cite every nuance and gradation; so specific, we can tell you who we'll be on any given day of the cycle. Take a number, any number, between one and twenty-eight.

Day Eleven on the calendar might read, for example, "breasts." This means that no sooner do you sit up in bed in the morning than both breasts send up alarming throbs of pain every time they move. It also means they are suddenly way, way bigger, swelling in all directions like the one that chased Woody Allen over a hillside in *Everything You Always Wanted to Know About Sex*. It means that your bra strains grotesquely to contain them. Now, one might think enlarged breasts are fun, in a Dolly Parton kind of way, but the soreness obviates much of that pleasure. It only gets worse 'til the end of the cycle. If you hug someone during that time, you feel like two nail-spiked volleyballs have come between you, and you bite your lip to keep from howling in pain.

Day Thirteen might read, "ate and drank." Ah, God: pitiful. This means, to be quite blunt, an appetite like Godzilla's. It means that on the way home from dinner somewhere, you have to stop for dinner. It means washing that food back with lots of wine or beer or whatever's within reach, and dessert, and no matter if you are distended like a pregnant woman by then, you are still desperate for some element of nourishment that is still missing, or else hasn't been invented yet. And trying to sleep thereafter can mean nightmares, and nightsweats, and off we go, on the roller coaster of hormone horror.

Let us dwell briefly on the simple notation, "night sweat." This does not mean a delicate film of moisture on the troubled woman's upper lip. It means waking up soaked. Sheets, blankets, pajamas. You stagger from the bed, wondering whether you've sleepwalked into the ocean. It ain't restful. And what, you gasp, if a lover has to experience this with you? How do you warn him about it? "Um—would you mind wrapping yourself in this towel before we turn in, honey? Never know when the roof might leak."

The worst of it is the crushing depression and irritability that accelerates right along with breast size. (By this time you've gained a waterballoon little belly, big enough to stash a small portable typewriter in. You can't easily zip your jeans closed.) Day after day of this. "Sad. Low. Awful. Fat. Badly depressed." Those are the words that can be repeated here; others tend toward the more—vivid, shall we say.

Not long ago (Day Twenty-three) I nearly murdered a young man at the corner grocery because his store had run out of that Sunday's *New York Times*. I'd considered myself a perfectly rational being until the kid looked around and scratched his head sleepily. Gee, they'd sold out, he guessed, and as he gestured vaguely down the street toward the next nearest newsstand, I saw that hapless boy as the true essence of human incompetence and stupidity. I was dumbfound with rage, felt the bile screaming along my veins. A *newspaper*, I told myself. On a beautiful Sunday morning. So you take a few more minutes, get it elsewhere. What in hell's wrong with you?

No question what's wrong. It's the same thing that bubbles up buckets of tears—over a piece of music, a passage in a book, a sliced tangerine, even television commercials, for God's sake, like the one showing the college kid arriving home early Christmas morning, or the sweet grandma telephoning her American family from the old country. Catch a snippet of *An American in Paris* and you are dead meat, racing for the Kleenex.

Every month commences with a subtle unease, which gives way to melancholy, which flows into sorrow, then despair, then builds to something like psychotic emergency—until, finally, that amazing moment when the pituitary gives its mysterious signal, and you literally feel the bad stuff lifting away like a dirty fog. I can tell you what I was doing at those moments, they are so vivid to me. One afternoon I was in the laundromat eating eggplant salad, resigned to a life of blurry gloom, and suddenly, clear as a bell I felt the Evil Thing simply lift up and fly away. As if a bad ghost had just fled my body. It's an extraordinary feeling, a clean glowing lightness. Hallelujah. Then you remember. Some people get to feel this good all the time. Why do I so strongly suspect they have penises?

It's not as though I haven't tried to take charge. I exercise like a maniac, take vitamins, drink various herbal teas. I try to eat smarter. I went to my doctors. Both work for a local medical group and, with all respect, they are overworked, late for everything, and sort of generically exhausted. These doctors are courteous, but overwhelmed. Unless your hair is on fire, they haven't much choice but to handle you like another stray presented at the animal shelter. My general practitioner, a mother of three, nodded wearily as she listened to my complaints, then quick as a bunny wrote me a prescription for a diuretic, murmuring something about more vitamin B_6. I tried to explain to her I took every vitamin known in our solar system but she was already out the door, late to everything for the next decade. I took the diuretic a couple of days but it made my bladder and kidneys feel shaky and urgent, like they were locked in fast-forward. I stopped the diuretic and turned to my gynecologist, a woman very near my age. I asked about hormone therapy. She shrugged. "We don't know that much about it yet," she admitted cheerfully. It's also possibly risky, she pointed out, perhaps linked with increased incidence of uterine cancer. Lovely: take your estrogen, and feel pretty and chipper on your way to chemotherapy.

I know this sounds trite, but I have the strongest hunch that a simple, effective antidote exists right under our noses that no one's hit upon yet. Something as simple as a weed growing wild in a vacant lot. And this leads me to wonder. What if, starting from their most vital years, men could count on eighteen to twenty days a month of pure teeth-gnashing, evil-twin personality, balloon-body anguish? What if this syndrome of suffering were built into their very genes, programmed to get worse with age, and that no matter what men did—acupuncture, hypnosis, macrobiotics, homeopathy, injections with the amniotic fluid of Swiss sheep—nothing could really help or change it? And suppose their misery were defined in medical circles as a cluster of amorphous symptoms, probably psychosomatic? Suppose that men were finally expected to endure being bloated, suicidal zombies for three-quarters of each month for the rest of their lives? Might that speed the finding of a cure?

Walk on, walk on with hope in your heart.
Guys, you can come back to this page now.
What, us? Oh, fine, thanks. Everything's fine—now.

Happy Evolutions

*N*OVELIST Ann Beattie came through town a few years ago, and from time to time I smile to remember the newspaper interview she gave. Beattie has gained a reputation over the years for characters, in her short stories and novels, who tend to muck around in queasily unresolved situations. They keep secrets, drift away, damage themselves and each other. Rarely do her players give us reason to believe they'll evolve happily. In the course of her talk with a local reporter, Beattie was asked the inevitable question about source material, and how it ranked against some prevailing idea of a rather more wholesome, or at least optimistic, view of modern American life.

I have never forgotten her blunt response: "Most of my friends live strange, complicated lives."

I thought, thank God.

For as we trade stories about ourselves and the people we know, my friends and I are continually astonished that the pool of evidence surpasses all reckoning: Most of us live strange, complicated lives.

Examples? One woman has been contentedly conducting an affair with two married men (presumably on different shifts) for the last twenty years. Another has been very satisfied to share her bisexual lover with his male lover for a decade.

I know of two men this year, gifted artists each, who are glad to serve as biological fathers to two lesbian couples' babies. Little work, lots of glory.

And let's see if I can cite this correctly: One lesbian's ex-husband and his new wife have just had a baby, whose ecstatic daycare providers are—you guessed it, this gay woman and her longtime live-in lover. The baby is adored as if she were the Second Coming, and in a manner of speaking, I suppose she is.

I know of several May-December marriages that radiate bliss, in which the *women* take the December roles. I know two couples who switched spouses, like tennis doubles or square dancing; all four remain cheerful friends some twenty years later. One friend of mine married the man she'd been visiting for years in prison. Several years after his release, they may be happier than anyone I've seen.

Some couples still keep what are called open marriages, allowing him, or her, or both to investigate other lovers. Many live apart half the week, the month, or the year. One woman prefers being the occasional lover to a man in a distant city, who is kept busy there placating two possessive girlfriends. She claims she likes being spared all the accumulated flotsam of jealousy: where he is, when he'll call.

And we haven't even begun to talk about the children of these arrangements. Plenty of kids in this nation go back and forth between reconfigurations of families and schedules that would baffle a physicist. Some children cross the street every other week to the co-family or parent; others cross several continents.

These stories would seem to defy what our media stubbornly and relentlessly continue to depict as ground-zero—traditional and exclusive marriages, couples and family units still overwhelmingly heterosexually oriented (though that is beginning to blur in official light, bit by bit). Debates rage on and off the page about the good or bad of modern relational inventions. Maybe in a century or so the smoke will have cleared, and we'll have some perspective. All that is certain now is that the old models are being retooled, and that sometimes the new arrangements work, and sometimes they explode.

What, for example, does the woman decide when her bi-sexual lover's male partner dies of AIDS, and now her lover, too, begins to show symptoms? Does the caretaking he will likely require until his last breath, fall automatically to her?

What of the woman who rears her live-in mate's two children by another marriage virtually from infancy, and at the moment the children are grown and out the door, he leaves her for a younger woman? Suppose she then finds a marvelous new man, who soon begins to indicate he wants to have a baby with her?

The wonder is that despite such stunning complexity, people continue to take risks, to hope for happy evolutions. They keep loving, getting married, having babies one way or another. But don't mail out your Hallmark cards just yet.

It strikes me that however unconventionally we undertake it, there is an extraordinary, consummate recklessness in any choice to love, because we are signing ourselves on for so much that is absolutely unknowable, with such potential for excoriating pain. The minute we love, there is a sea-change—the whole picture becomes fertilized like a zygote, imploding and effervescing with instant chemical foment—and our life, and all the lives touching it, ripple and spin like those wildly flipping airport monitors of arrivals and departures—and nothing, count on it, nothing, will ever be the same. Choosing this person at that time packs, for better or worse, as thundering a wallop to a person's destiny as a move to Calcutta, or experiencing a death. (You take on a death, when you take on a life.)

Did the woman who loved the bisexual man deprive herself of the opportunity to meet someone more "appropriate," who might not have died so soon? If the woman who spent six difficult, but very rich, years of her thirties with a married man had been wise enough to get out of it while she was younger, would she have found a healthier love, and lived out an entirely different existence? Though people rack themselves with this kind of second-guessing hindsight, in the end it's as useless as asking whether we should have breathed a certain way on a certain day ten years ago. Woody Allen got a big part of it right, when he named our prime rationale—"the heart wants what it wants"—though unfortunately, out of his mouth in his then-circumstances, the line sounded like self-serving childishness.

Americans may indeed invite accusations of childishness, criticism that we are still driven by naive romanticism. Even so, I wonder whether the odd liaisons we forge may be among the last ways we allow ourselves—caged in our fine-mesh grids of agendas—to fully inhabit the present. To engage in time in a way that forgets time, a mindfulness larger and richer and more urgent, and at the same time more pristine, cropped of constraining webs of past and future, slipped from its customary harness of accountability. This is not to defend the damage we cause. It may be useful to remember one definition of romanticism in literature: passion made more vivid by its own imbedded doom.

Yet no matter how avant or freewheeling we may style ourselves, the fundamental things still seem to apply. As a rule, people don't go looking for "arrangements." We look to be beloved, we look to connect—if possible, with a big bang. And that is not shameful. But we may feel subtly haunted or indicted by the breach between ideal and real, as we strike bargains or devise alternatives, when connection falls short. And there is the shame, and the tyranny.

Because the fact is most of us still push off, in our inmost thinking, from some variation of the "four myths of relationship" suggested by author Daphne Rose Kingma—that romantic partnerships should be "daily, domestic, exclusive, and forever." Or that families be as balanced and serene as the ones in 1950s ads for kitchen appliances. And by comparison with those standards, what really goes on will always look, and feel, creepingly deviant.

Strange, complicated lives.

Somebody Help Me

*D*EAR Smart 'n Sensible Pantyhose Manufacturers:

I never write letters to manufacturers unless it is the last straw. Last time I wrote anybody was when I found an actual metal bolt in a package of sourdough dinner rolls. The bolt was neatly baked into one of the rolls, and I felt it in a biteful of bread. I sent the bolt back to the manufacturer with a letter. *What a fool.* I could have retired on the money I'd have been awarded for emotional and teeth damage. (As it happened I had not bitten down hard on the thing. But suppose I had. Suppose I had cracked a filling. Suppose I had swallowed the goddamn thing. Women are incredibly meek, as a rule, don't you think? Doesn't it actually amaze you when you add it up, how meek we are in general? The way we always say I'm sorry when someone else bumps into us, the way we buy things because they are packaged in red and yellow, or because they have a smell we remember from when our mama hung out the wash when we were four?) I bet those sourdough executives sent a nasty little memo to all their trembling underlings. I bet they toasted each other on having got off so easily that time, thanks to the incredible stupidity of another female consumer. Heidi out of the Alps, that's me.

So this is to return the enclosed $3.69-plus-tax product, your sheer-to-waist, Sublime Soirée, Midnight Smoke pantyhose. I wore them twice, and as I pulled them on the second time, I watched a hole shred open at the belly and run straight down one thigh.

I was late to work, and it was the last pair in the drawer. When this happens, it is difficult not to experience it as a bad omen.

You should understand some things right away. I am five-foot-four and weigh about 125 pounds. So don't feel you can point to size as a determining factor in the ripping of the product. It says quite clearly on the package: Medium to Tall. I have always felt relieved to fall into the Medium to Tall category. The chart on the back demonstrating the heights and weights that fall within Medium to Tall covers a very large turf. It makes a kind of jagged shape, shaded in dark red so you can easily track the inner and outer boundaries of Medium to Tall. A red lightning bolt, or glacier, is what it looks like, crowded with statistics, coated with them like black ants. And my five-four-125 can tuck right into the middle of that big chunk of data, inside all those other little numbers and inches, causing me to actually feel *moderate* about my size. Ask any woman what this means to her, no matter if she's president. Ask her.

I did not machine-launder the hose, as you caution against on your label. But I was going to, if you must know. Because to tell you the truth I always throw the hose into the laundry. I know it wears them out faster. *For longer lasting wear, hand-wash separately in warm water and mild soap. Drip dry. Do not bleach.* But Smart 'n Sensible people, work with me here. Say a woman hacks through an office day of interruptions and dead-lines and phone calls, one of them mentioning that the nine-year-old has cut his head open during recess in such a way that one piece of his eyebrow is in one place and another in another. And say the ex-husband has driven the boy to emergency to be stitched up, but announces to her he will not pay the insurance deductible. Say this woman claws her way to and from home every day through sna-king traffic, a limitless horizon of glinting metal with the faces of corpses at all those steering wheels—say she does this for so much of her waking time she begins to feel that instead of being born she must have somehow been manifested one day, fully-grown, in the act of driving a Toyota hatchback. And say the radio is nothing but shrieking ads and she is risking her safety in that traffic to lower her eyes in search of the bloody volume button. Say she has $24 left in the bank and it is ten days to payday and the only thing in the house to eat is instant soup. Say the baby looks at her sadly in the morning because he now understands that her familiar words "Right back" mean she will be late again to pick him up from daycare. Say she is carrying one and holding the other by the hand as they ease their way toward the front door and just then all the groceries fall out of the passenger side of the car and the precious bottle of wine breaks; she can see it soaking through the brown bag onto the sidewalk, and all she can think is *why is everything so hard; somebody help me.* Say she finally feeds and bathes and consoles and beds her children and puts the rooms in some kind of order and it is perhaps 11:30 at night, and she knows she will have to rise at 5:00. We are talking about a *twenty-year emergency;* we are talking about taking three aspirin with the glass of wine, and you are talking about *hand-wash separately in warm water and mild soap.* I don't even *iron,* please understand.

Do any other women write to tell you they feel *just* a mite foolish when they pull on these diaphanous gizmos with the strip up the crotch, that stay unpunctured for so little time? You look at yourself in the mirror wearing them, and you wonder. So few of us in this world really look like the women who model them, those reedy, coltish things who seem about to float away. I see the big photos of them in the bus stops and on the sides of the buildings in town. I look at them, and I must tell you, there is this moment, just a moment, of real awfulness, because I think about how I look compared with the way they look. Now, if I am a smart and reasonably alright to look at person, how do people feel when they see those ads who are not too smart or not really too wonderful to look at, I often wonder. Smart 'n Sensible people, our city has a very bad graffiti problem, and I must tell you something a little embarrassing about that. I *love* it when the graffiti kids leave their work on these models. I love seeing those creamy, triumphant vampires, smirking at you one day from this golden eternity of female ravishingness—and next day, staring at you jagged and disoriented, raunchy with black and blue and red mustaches and broken teeth, a kind of hysterical tattooing, motley clumps of initials in wonderful bruising colors all over their arms and cleavages and pretty summer dresses. Pretty girls transforming into Hitler. It makes me glad the kids are alive enough in the crazy world to say so.

At $3.69 a pair, I cannot let it go this time. Less, I could let go of, maybe, but I never seem to have enough cash on me to be able to act nonchalant about $3.69, no matter how I try. I know it costs you maybe 29¢ to produce them. But I respect that you must pay your employees; some of them must be women like me. I buy those Sublime Soirées to keep my legs warm, to help them look like what our little blink of time on earth calls womanly—and because your logo tells me I am not an idiot for doing so. It says *designed so you look and feel terrific for all your special occasions. It says you know you are getting great value.* And so we all do it again and again, buying them and shredding them and buying them, hoping for shapely health and liberty, hoping for some gentle prince or poet, intoxicated by Midnight Smoke, to slip an arm around us and whisper *let us go then for champagne, your children can play with my children, I like you better bare-legged,* at the foot of a series of shimmering Parisian fountains. And so I am returning this ripped bit of synthetic webbing for a new one, a new shot at it, a message in a bottle tossed to sea, trading in the torn dream for a smart and sensible replacement.

Womb Mates

*S*HE WAS conceived and formed in the same space I was. Now that that space is gone, she is a kind of living testament: the only being who can corroborate my own memories—that what I believe happened, in fact did.

I watched in amazement when they brought her home, a lump of something in a blanket, about the size of a loaf of bread. I fetched her clean diapers for our mother. It never occurred to me to hate her.

I taught her to speak. We sat on the floor in the mote-swirled sunlight through the screen door as I patiently made her repeat: Yellow. *Lellow.* Spaghetti. *Basketti.* Hamburger. *Hangabur.* Her limbs emerged plump from her clean playsuit, her hair flew in soft light brown feathers from her head like a little wren's, and her deep brown eyes smiled at me, that button face a study in gentle equanimity.

We faced each other on the floor, playing jacks, marbles, crayons; mapped out worlds, stories, families thriving in cheerfully idiosyncratic straits. We stood facing each other on the back-yard swings, swooping from side to side, a human sandwich for a giant to eat, singing songs to lure the giant. We bellowed the Davy Crockett theme in the public restrooms with good acoustics, so we could hear our echoes. She was a tough little cowboy then in jeans and boots, the brown mane yanked back by a hairpin on either side. She squinted and fussed when my father tried to pose us for his brownie camera, because those were the days when you had to face the light, and she hated the sun in her eyes. I do not remember a single fight—only the time she jumped out from behind a wall to scare me, and succeeded. I cried.

She grew into a knockout brunette, boys trailing her through high school and ever after. Even now, with a fat grinning baby in her arms and a small child at each side, men stop what they are doing to admire her. I smile and shake my head, but there's nothing mysterious about it, for she is invitingly rounded and sensuous, with kind light in her eyes. She married young, was widowed young, and as soon as she could walk upright again in the world of men, they floated after her like bees for summer flowers. She married again, and then once more, now a hardworking mother and secretary in a bustling Sierra Nevada town. Her house is full of food, noise, games and toys, laughter. The refrigerator is pasted with photos of the kids, animals, friends, fathers, and me.

I have taken shelter in that house for twenty years, from whatever world I was building or fleeing, from Africa, Europe, the South Pacific, from lost loves and lost jobs and new jobs and new loves. When I arrive vibrating and numb after the long drive, there is always food and wine, medicines and teas, and best of all, three smoldering young faces with three urgent reports to make. She and I look at each other, and know we won't be able to finish a sentence until much later that night. I have slept on the floor, on the couch, in the kids' beds—always made fresh for me, under the extra blankets she always remembers to lay over. The dog tries to stash himself underneath the bed, so he won't be exiled to the cold garage, and he wakes me too early with a cold nose in my neck and a plaintive *Rowwwr* to be let out. The baby will wake then in the next room, composing his own songs aloud for a while, until one of the boys also wakes and goes to him, climbing into the crib with him, where he will proceed to teach the littler one to speak—they face each other, smiling. *Lellow. Basketti.*

From my bed in the kids' room I put aside my magazine and stare at the posters of Joe Montana, Will Clark, Michael Jordan slam-dunking the very moon into a cosmic basket. I stare at the pennants, the photos of ski teams and soccer teams, class portraits, Tai Kwon Do certificates, boxes of baseball cards, the entire Hardy Boys series lined up in careful sequence, trophies, sacks of multi-colored paintballs, catalogues of motocross gear which have gradually replaced Ninja Turtles. Surrounded by the icons of the boys' budding lives, all the possibility and yearning and dailiness of them seeped into the very walls, I am consoled as I would be nowhere else. I'm related to these guys. I'm safe here.

She made this home, and she made these children. And in the end it is her very essence that binds all this together, that makes the rooms snug and welcoming as a fresh-made, warmly-blanketed bed. If she left us, God forbid, it would all collapse into cold ash. We know it is the sheer force of her will, the fertility of her heart's imagination, that carves a field of home-ness out of the anarchy of our random lives, her determination alone that buttresses and furnishes and defends this turf with passion and tenderness. We follow her from room to room, the kids and I.

She does not resemble me in specific features—hers are more pert, far prettier, and I have always been relieved to insist it—if there's going to be a beautiful woman stealing the spotlight, I want it to be her. But we are alike in an aura about the face and body, a positioning of bones, a symmetry of hands, coloration, and very much, in voice. When she says "hello" into the phone, that compassionate lilt in the last syllable, my heart squeezes and my throat constricts, because her voice is like a long-distance echo of our father's burgundy cello tones, our mother's fluid, golden violin. She is Andrea Frank Starkey Havens Carabetta, widow, divorcée, happily married mother of three boy-children, all of whom look like a slightly scrambled version of our father, who never lived to know they would exist. She is my only family, my mother, my daughter, source of all safety and sweetness. She is my sister.

We could not be more different. She is country, I am city. She is domestic, her house packed with lush cushions and plants and crystal, her pantry full of tantalizing and comforting possibility. I am a distracted bachelor with a $130 stereo, a few faded posters and what she and I call a mass murderer's refrigerator. She reads potboilers and adores suspense movies; I receive weekly New Yorkers like eucharist, and run from the room when blood is shed on the television screen. The contrast is piquant: nurturing home-maker, bookish ascetic—yet we tap from the same emotional reserve. By now we know and anticipate one another so easily, so deeply, we unthinkingly finish each other's sentences, and often speak in code. No one else knows what I mean so exquisitely, painfully well; no one else knows so exactly what to say, to fix me. One day I told her I was having terrible, inexplicable dread—waves of panic and existential horror such that even the quality of the *daylight* made me reel with fear and queasiness. In an instant, she nailed the malady and soothed me the way an expert calms an agitated animal. (Diagnosis: mild PMS, slightly hung over, needing sleep, carrot juice, aspirin, and vitamin C. One night's good rest will flush away this horror, she declared—and it did.)

Say my eyes light up to see a certain kind of soft, oversized plaid shirt in one of the winter gear stores we roam during holiday breaks—and say we then go on about our lives: What do you suppose awaits me under the tree Christmas morning, long after I'd forgotten my longing? If my birthstone happens to be opal, and she's divined I associate powerful magic with that beautiful gem, whom do you suppose presents me with my first opal ring?

It works both ways: we take turns. I send her vitamins, Bailey's Irish Cream, sexy blouses, luxury moisturizers and hair conditioners, earrings shaped like dangling moons and stars, roses made of painted seashells, magazines of science and archaeology, because those are her delights. When she went through her New Mexico phase I plied her with coyote-and-cactus gimcracks from Santa Fe. Our mutual efforts to please are shameless, and people seldom grasp the mightiness of it, the raw instinct, the unabashed sentiment. When there is an earthquake, when *Around the World in Eighty Days* shows up on TV, when I sell a story, fall in love, skin a knee—I'm on the phone to her. When the middle child splits his eyebrow in two, when the eldest gets straight A's or into big trouble, when the baby is witty, when she's read a passage or heard a joke or eaten something she adored, she's dialing me up. Last week she coaxed the baby to sing "Take Me Out to the Ballgame" on my message machine. All I can offer, by way of baffled explanation: We're all we have.

I am very grateful to her husband and children, not least for loving her and making her glad, but also for accommodating my fierce bond with her, the oldest bond either of us will ever know, longer and in many ways larger than a marriage, yet full of unapologetic romance. It goes so impossibly deep, it seems to reach into places neither of us understands—into dreamlife. We dream of each other, we dream of the children, we dream of our parents and the house we came up in. We talk of it to ease the intensity. It is as if our cells remember that their beginnings were intertwined. I have styled myself lifelong as a strict agnostic, but as we age, that softens. Perhaps we hovered together like co-mingled vapors in some anteroom before we became earthly, and perhaps we will after earthliness, as well.

I am not sure all this is very typical.

Other people, as I understand it, have fights and feuds and estrangements with their grown siblings; store up resentments over gaffes great and small, refuse to speak to each other for years, even disavow the other's existence. Some simply have nothing to say to each other. This is inconceivable to me, as it is to her. You can suggest it is because we were caught together, as children—perhaps our souls were soldered together then—in the Pompeii-like moment of losing a mother, and a father not long thereafter. Maybe, and maybe not. Many orphaned children grow up with no particular affinity for one another. You can call us neurotic, compensatory, co-dependent. Fine.

Whatever it is, it is *formed*. No question that this woman who was a soft-feathered baby and then a radiant coed and then an athlete and adventuress, who whispered goodbye to her first young husband in a hospital morgue, who with her next built a boat from the trunk of a single giant redwood that would sail to the Marquesas, and then built a house to live in, who three times let doctors slice open her belly to lift out a fine new son—this woman who came after me from a womb long-gone, shares with me now a hopeless and irrational urgency about the use of time, which of course translates as life on earth. A wakefulness in time, an embracing of time—a galvanic shiver of awe for the fact that the two little girls in the black-and-white snapshots even made it this far. Awe for the shabby sanctity of the mountain house, for the stately procession of seasons, of husbands and lovers and kids, for the suburban rituals, the struggle to pay bills, the video games and lentil burritos and Desinex and microwave baby bottles—for the whole, brief, wheeling galaxy of fireworks, which can scarcely be told, but must be lived. I pray we get old together.

Notes from a Solstice

MY YOUNG co-worker just burst out of her office wearing The Look again.

Eyes aflame, lips tight, she charges past me to the typewriter and savagely cranks an envelope into the carriage. I know she's just hung up on her ex-husband.

She whirls to face me.

"If any of your friends ever complain to you about being single and childless," she begins, in a tone of such clenched control that it sounds tender, "tell them that they are blessed with their freedom."

Go on, I offer, making myself very still.

Her voice rises. "Because having to deal with the shrapnel of divorce—with a child between you—creates this—huge—thing," she gasps. "A thing that you're burdened and belabored with for the rest of your life!"

She's ready to go on *Oprah*. Don't do it, don't do any of it, she scowls. My colleague cherishes her little girl, of course, but the price is gut-busting. What you have is bliss, she informs me. What she has, she asserts crisply, is hell.

I know she's right. Not only do I have ample evidence—friends and relatives everywhere dealing painfully with ex-mates who are their children's parents. But I also happen to be distancing myself from parenthood, a grad student in the School of Curmudgeon. Which is to say, I'm older. The temptation she warns me against is slipping the bonds of its prime-time slot. I'm getting settled in my ways, attached to comfy routines—I, who slept in pastures, stowed away on charter planes, made my morning toilette in gas station restrooms; I, whose every earthly belonging could once fit behind the backseat of VW Bug.

I love pure silence now, and the fact that I can have a grapefruit or three orders of chow mein for dinner, stay up late, run at dawn, come and go as I please. I am passing through a kind of solstice, from a time when the craving for mamapapababy pulled me the way the Sirens pulled Ulysses, or the moon pulls the tides. For various reasons, I escaped the sucking vortex called Making a Family, that most humans do hard time in. Once this was sorrowful loss. Now I'm thankful for my solitude.

Even so, every time a baby enters the picture—in a basket, on a shoulder—heaven help me, I do that thing that women do. "Oh, look," I breathe. "A new baby." Everything stops—except the overpowering urge to go directly to the infant, put my nose to its fat, velvety, melted-candy-smelling little neck and inhale deeply, murmuring and nuzzling.

It's a reflex. Even my bitter office-mate still goes gooey at the sight of babies. Most women do, except those just released from mommy prison. "Doesn't do a thing for me," snapped a recent dinner companion, who has just finished rearing two. She took one look at the holy infant being paraded through the restaurant and jerked her head back around so fast that I thought it would snap off. Here was clarity. Here was certainty. Here was burnout.

For me, it's come to this: When I phone my best friend, who tells me her mothers' group scolded her for feeding her son politically incorrect juice, whose big weekend consists of visiting her parents (because they can help), who over a tinkly music box apprises her little cosmic gift, "No no, mustn't slug Mommy in the face,"—suddenly I am biting my lip to keep from announcing my apartment's just caught fire so I can hang up quickly, in case you can get pregnant from talking to a mother on the phone.

I'm saying the bloom is off the reproductive rose, and it's not so bad. Being a doting auntie is as close as I now care to come. Yes, it sounds loutishly self-satisfied, and no, children are not to be mused over like the merits of clip-on earrings. I never thought I'd be saying this, but go ahead and have your rich epiphanies that you wouldn't trade for immortal life. I'll be in the stands, waving.

And yet I now see why it is still probably better to have the babies young. Even if you do end up in six or seven years slamming the phone down daily on your ex, your stomach's knots in knots as you cajole and browbeat the fool you once swore you'd spend your life with to cough up those support payments.

When else would you have had the energy?

No Boundaries

I SAW HER again this weekend.

The one I'm thinking of wanders down my street once in a while. This time she stopped in at the laundromat where I was washing my clothes. She comes in, scoops up whatever newspapers have been abandoned, pauses to read the notices on the laundromat bulletin board, and shuffles out—twice she's performed this ritual, while I was there. Perhaps in her late fifties, she could be anyone's grandmother or aunt. She wears a sweater, skirt, thick corrective shoes; she is stout, her face leathery; her legs swollen and veined. But it's the expression in her eyes which most upsets me. There is effort in those eyes to show that things are making sense. Her eyes scan the streets and shop windows in a way one imagines she believes purposeful, intentional, having snappy business to attend. Yet behind that brave squint she is visibly frightened, restive, lonely; visibly aware she has nowhere to go, and nothing to do.

There are people worse off than her. I'm pretty sure she eats, and has a place to live, though the particulars of these conditions may by anyone else's standards be sad, or strange.

But here's the truly awful thing. Part of me is irritated by her ruse. Part of me wants to say: *You don't fool me. I know you're not really completely knit together, not part of the scene. I know you're lost. Just go be busy at lostness somewhere out of my sight.*

I am sickened by my own involuntary, mob-mentality reaction—not least because I fear being myself one day at the receiving end of it.

I am terrified of becoming her.

Specifically, I do not believe there is huge distance between what she is, or appears to be, and what I am. Certainly not much stands between us materially. I rent an apartment, own a car, work a job. But I wince with the appearance of each new study intoning how one grave illness, accident, or fire can put any of us into the street in a twinkling. The math of it is irrefutable: In a matter of months most of us would be bled dry.

But it isn't only thoughts of money or security that strike me so forcefully about what connects me to the woman in the laundromat. Looking at her reminds me of the delicacy of belief and engagement—of our faithful, wakeful participation in the weave of life. I think about the ephemerality of will and wit and verve, of the clear-eyed handclasp, arm-over-arm in the dizzying Virginia Reel of modern commerce: the grid of it, its laws and codes and mores. *Compos mentis*, is the legal term: Somebody's home, and the lights are on. The strong handshake, the crisp registry in the eyes, the words spoken with equanimity—all taken for granted, until those instances when we note, with instant alarm, their absence.

A friend once told me that following a nervous breakdown some years ago, she remembers it was very difficult for her to read the newspaper. In that period, she recalls, she had "no boundaries";

her whole being would flow into, or fuse with, the ghastly news reports. Her ability to individuate from the chaotic stream was temporarily lost, so that her sense of self tended to empty out unrestrained into the stories she read—a kind of psychic hemophilia. Perhaps when we look at people in that foggy region between destitution and compos mentis, we remember our own nearness to that blanketing fog. We believe that if we are vigilant and determined and wary enough, we won't become enshrouded, carried off by it. I don't know that it works that way.

Most of us have known what it is to want to hide from the impatient traffic of the world; forced to face it in low moments, we cringe. In those moments I imagine looking out from the laundromat woman's eyes—on a heedless, clamorous scene; slightly familiar, slightly menacing. She wanders the dreamscape, never feeling she has it quite in hand, never able to fully wake up. Maybe it is sleep itself that provides the woman, and those like her, some measure of relief.

Meantime, the rest of us jostle for position. We lay plans, believe in the possible. And we pray that our brains continue to percolate, that our health stays sturdy, that our eyes carry compassionate light—light that appears to make sense of things.

The Servant Thing

THE FILM CREW showed up on a Thursday morning, young, hip, and energetic. Their leader—I'll call him Michael—had arranged it by phone. They would borrow our third floor that day to interview a colorful, local politician. Michael strode out of the elevator and grasped my hand heartily. He was tall, boyish, flashing an ingratiating smile as his eyes shone: obviously accustomed to directing, he relished the challenge of a new venue. Our building clearly pleased him, with its terrific view of the city and all the facilities his crew could need, free of charge.

We chatted some moments. Young Michael (say he was pushing thirty) looked directly at me, addressing me in a lively, flawlessly professional way—as if I were a knowledgeable peer. I found this refreshing, because at my front-desk work, I am accustomed to being invisible to visiting VIPs—and mostly I prefer that; the anonymity ensures a certain privacy. But intrigued by his work, his intelligent warmth and vitality, I gladly showed Michael around, met his colleagues, helped them navigate their trucks into the garage and their equipment up the stairs; found them phones, arranged to page them with calls, to check for faxes, copy their papers, and so on. Later I patiently suggested local restaurants; ordered lunch for them on the phone, and, finally, since Michael didn't seem to have anyone to spare for the task, trotted around the corner with his personal check and identification cards to pick up the food.

But after it arrived, more orders and requests kept tumbling in. There wasn't enough rice with the meal. They needed more eggrolls. They were missing an iced coffee. They needed a receipt from the restaurant so they could deduct the lunch expense. Important calls and faxes were pending that had to be routed to them instantly. Somehow the politican to be interviewed had not located our front doorbell, and had gone home to phone the crew and complain he could not enter the building. And I swear I do not think I would have minded continuing to bat these balls had there not occurred, before my eyes, a strange transformation in the upbeat, genial Michael as the day wore on.

He got cocky. His easy egalitarianism had given way to curt demands. His bright eyes had dulled and would not meet my gaze. The change was gradual but distinct, and as my teeth began to grind I remembered, with dull shock, how many women face this level of address as part of their workday routine. Michael had decided my unlimited go-fer services were an office amenity. It was the queerest experience to witness at the same time as I acceded to it, happening so quickly I never seemed to find a good moment to halt it. But when Michael finally asked, quite coolly and pointedly, whether a new receipt for lunch had been procured, I thought: *enough*, and bluntly answered no. I wanted to smack him. *Listen*, brat, I wanted to say. You don't seem to get it. My help to you today was a gesture of hospitality. Ours is an equal opportunity office, and people here do their fair share.

That wouldn't have been a lie. My boss—a remarkable man, I admit—has not a moment's compunction about answering the phone, making coffee, picking up food, or hauling equipment, and neither does anyone else working here. The staff takes turns pitching in when the need's apparent. I know our situation's unusual, but come to think of it, most of the men I've ever really cared for have performed the bulk of their own chores, accepting help—or requesting it—graciously. Few have assumed they'd be served. When that arrogance seeps out of someone (like bad body odor), I notice a basic mortification—everyone in the room flinches just perceptibly (the same diminishment and embarrassment we feel when we come upon someone publicly browbeating someone). And I sense that people on the receiving end of such arrogance tend to regress to *exactly* the degree of sullenness, stupidity, or irresponsibility they are accused of—just as they also tend to rise to meet a larger, more generous expectation.

The moment that caught me off-guard, the moment that turned a small knife, was the dropping away of the mask. Michael had apparently targeted me as the individual who could get him what he needed. So he'd opened up the charm full throttle—then let it dry up once things were rolling, revealing the surly manipulator underneath. I'd swallowed the charm act whole, imagining it the overture of some enlightened new collective, and felt like an idiot for it.

Then I realized how lucky I was. A girlfriend who labors as a secretary for a busy medical organization quickly remarked, on hearing this story: "Of course, that's what I deal with every day." Worse yet, her bosses are women.

It has made me think twice as I gaze up at the looming ranks of office windows downtown. Are those rooms filled with that sort of action? Does the pay compensate? I don't make much money, but seldom must I cringe at some bigger gun's bidding;

rarely must I chant a lot of sycophantic yesses. Thus I forget, most of the time, how it feels to be ordered around. I'm not naive enough to pray the world suddenly banish its hierarchies of skills and services, or that we all commence to dance on eggshells around each other. But there are ways of working with people which do not demean them. The imperious young man reminded me that even temporarily playing the snapped-at servant doesn't feel good. It feels like some part of you is being held hostage.

What You See

SITTING DOWN to lunch with two female publishers on a brilliantly sunny day, we turned our attention to the waiter who'd approached our table and was cheerfully reciting the day's specials. We stopped all business and listened attentively.

He was perhaps twenty, the kind of beauty that is startling, the kind that causes double-takes: limpid gray-blue eyes beneath curling dark lashes, flawless skin the color of honey, tousled hair to match. Slightly androgynous. One imagined him the new beauty at Oxford, the treasure of an exclusive prep school, the kept fawn of a wealthy old satyr.

Aschenbach's obsession. The young man gazed at each of us calmly; clear and guileless as the buttery sun pouring through the restaurant windows that day. I stared after the serene fellow as he walked off. All three of us women shot one another quick looks, and the light dancing in three pairs of eyes was unmistakeable. The moment begged for punctuation. I shook my head and opened my hands to them, in a kind of helpless appeal for clemency.

"It's so distracting when they're that beautiful."

Both women laughed—but I scarcely heard them. The sun-drenched restaurant had suddenly dissolved, and I saw myself standing in my summer dress that tied up behind the neck and dipped low in front, at a tableful of tourists on the island of Maui—the Kihei Fish House, where I waitressed in my early twenties.

I needed the money, and was earnest by nature. So I'd stand there and strain to smile as the broad shots rained down around me.

"Are you on the menu?"

"Does your boyfriend approve of this?"

"If I order dessert, will you feed it to me?"—all accompanied by suggestive drooped-eyelids, waggling brows, conspiratorial winks and leers. These comments, like a sort of vaudeville warmup act, generally had to be danced to or applauded a bit before anyone would grant me the unutterable relief of ordering their meals.

The performers were most often paunchy married men who would then smirk 'round the table at their companions for approval—including their wives and girlfriends. The women, invariably, would offer me the brief, tight, stricken smile of conflicted loyalties: They regretted, but they forgave, and silently they hoped I would too.

I was taking my noon or sunset runs in those years at the local high school track, and I remember the remarks and sound effects addressed me from passing cars or pedestrians; witticisms most publications cannot quote in print. I ran in loose shorts and a firmly encasing Speedo swimsuit. It was hot in Hawaii. I was of zaftig build and painfully conscious of it, but quite strong and devoted to my hard workouts.

I remember how I struggled with the feelings ignited by the leers and catcalls. First, I was crazed with fury—but in those days (as now), even to allow eye contact, let alone answer back, was to invite grave danger. So I'd segué into lofty contempt: I was light-years beyond the mentalities of these hand-dragging cretins whose brains couldn't have been bigger than walnuts.

But in quieter moments, I reflected again and again how sad it was that I would never truly be seen by them. Seen—to my mind—meant to some degree, known. And not in the biblical sense. I was a daughter, sister, auntie, writer, musician, athlete, traveler. But for the jeering men, I could only be something unprintable.

Now I'm a forty-two-year-old woman who has just watched herself doing something that bears an alarming resemblance to leering—at the expense of an apparently sincere young man doing his job. (He had moved well away from us women by the time we laughed.)

Sometimes I think of it this way. When we were small, adults swooped down on us, embraced us too hard, pinched our cheeks, gawked at us and gushed, "Sweetheart, how you've grown!" I remember blinking up at them, thinking, "But I couldn't help it." Growing, to me, was as external and remote an event as weather. To be gushed over as if I were the agent of my growing entirely missed who I was: what I loved, feared, thought silly or important. Grownups meant well but were clueless, I sadly concluded.

In mind of this, I have tried to remember that to stare and fuss over someone as if they were the agent of their stunning beauty is not always useful. They may indeed be the agent of their beauty, and very anxious to succeed at it. But I have challenged myself, at least in preliminary courtesies, to try to speak to whoever might be living inside that gorgeous scaffolding—without a glint of irony.

Yet here's a confession of a lower order. Now that I'm not

as often the object of the leering I so bitterly despised in my twenties, I feel a little disoriented and dismayed. Heads don't turn as predictably when I walk down the street or through a room. Salesclerks are brisk and respectful, instead of flirting and gaping. More of the people I deal with daily are younger than I. And when they do stare, there is a subtle but distinct unsavoriness about it—something steamy and unseemly.

I may remain firm and curvy, but my face shows wear, my eyes more complex light; streaks of silver wink from my dark hair. It's fascinating, and a bit horrifying. In low moments I think of Blanche duBois in *Streetcar*. The young woman who once scorned cracks about her dishiness (one colleague declared, "When I think of Joan, I think of going into a Bavarian forest and breathing deeply")—that woman now wonders whether she comes off as a specimen wandering around in a slip with the strap falling, sweat beading up between her breasts, pining for the vague redemption of some grunting Brando. Spare me!

I see now there was a certain luxury in the lofty contempt we guarded so fiercely in our twenties. One felt smug and powerful believing oneself luscious and untouchable and brainy, all at once. Granted, this smug sense of power didn't much change the fifty cents we were paid to any man's dollar, or the fact that we may have had to ward off unwanted advances (or, more tragically, succumb to them) to get work done or degrees earned.

In fact, these realities fed the feeling of invincible superiority. Maybe it was only the predictable arrogance of youth and beauty. But one ideal did hold—the notion that validity might be measured by how much we felt known.

Two days later I stayed up late watching an epic documentary about the making of *Gone With the Wind*. Hours of footage opened wide the private lives and loves of all the principals. There they were, mugging on the sets and at gala dinners, gamboling on lawns, pouting and preening and flirting: Vivien Leigh, all chiseled alabaster and raven hair; her lover, Laurence Olivier, nearly Greek in male perfection; wry-rogue Clark Gable and his platinum Carole Lombard; creamy Olivia de Havilland; winsome and dashing Leslie Howard; even big raffish David Selznick, who somehow (Benzedrine, and a monomaniacal will) commandeered the whole leaky ship of a film to shocking success.

Mesmerized by their phosphorescent images in my dark living room, I slowly forgot, despite the fashions and props, that the era was 1939. They were real to me: the exquisite, vibrant Leigh clowning by the swimming pool with her suave, boyish Olivier, picking hibiscus from Hollywood bushes, gliding and glittering out of propellered airplanes and limousines into premieres and Academy Awards parties.

And then these people became old.

Selznick and Leigh emerge from a plane in the early '60s: He is gray, jowly, rheumy-eyed; she is wizened and puffy—bitterlooking. Both would be dead in a few years; Gable not long thereafter. The magnificent Olivier in taped interviews before his death was shrunken, frail, wattled, desperately unwell—if still elegant and droll—a quaking old man. "It can't be," I heard myself murmur, staring at the TV screen transfixed, appalled. "It can't."

Ah, it can, and it shall. To me, to you. To the lovely young man in the restaurant. We must learn the lesson again and again, remember it only in small doses, little moments, because it's easiest on us that way. We must marvel, and mourn a bit each time. It may not be news. But like every increment of revelation along the continuum, when it happens to us, it *is* new.

I'm So Happy
for You

A FRIEND BROUGHT HIM to town for dinner. I'd heard of him, was all; when we shook hands, I noted only that he had a kind face. We had dinner, another dinner, and the rest is not history, but ongoing. I did not at first dare believe it could work, but as various positive clues turned up, I started to dare. And over time, to my amazed joy, indeed it's taken shape and color, blooming into a lovely, healthy living thing.

I still proceed with rapt care. It has been a long time since I was in love, and I'm determined to be better at it, to relearn a lot from scratch. Like the fact (surprise, surprise) that no relationship is ever a "done deal"—not folded tidily in a drawer like an insurance policy or set of long underwear, as if once installed, you can dust your hands and turn to other business. Instead the love is animate, breathing, growing, mega-faceted, moody, and vulnerable, requiring enormous respect and tender care—which very often means stepping back to give it room.

But the aspect of this event that was least foreseeable, and that has proved most prickly, is telling people about it.

The irony's on me, because for so long I've been the one who congratulated others. My immediate feelings at those times were seldom generous, though I labored to sound generous. *How wonderful for you,* I'd say. *It's terrific, marvelous; I am so happy for you.* I'd hope my smile looked more like a smile than a wince, for there was no denying the little stab I felt, a puncturing somewhere deep behind the solar plexus.

I knew perfectly well that self-pity was a disastrously selfish and rude response, so I did all I could to conceal or expunge it. Sometimes I would say—truthfully—that my friend's good news proved such things were still possible in an arid, anarchic world. I gave myself sharp little scoldings, reminding myself that people finding each other was part of the rich serendipity of life, rather awesome amid all the pain and drudgery—and that even if one were not presently having that part of it (or even believing much in it), one wanted finally to be included in the weave of it, to grasp it, to love the tableau. The peace that passeth all understanding comes soon enough, right?

So I would go away after congratulating the lucky one, and mull it over. Eventually I would come to feel happy for the couple, as well as (somewhat clinically) curious how they'd evolve. If they "kept on it," deepened with it—I was impressed. And eventually the reconfigured constellation of that couple would take its place in my galaxy, until one day I'd have difficulty remembering how it was before they got together.

Now, though, I recognize the flicker across some faces when I tell them I am seeing someone. Or I hear something in their voices, even in letters. Some reactions have been churlish—notably from certain male friends. Sometimes they just murmur a mild pleasantry, and then I do not hear from them again for long, long stretches. Others say things I'm sure they mean to sound like friendly caveats, but in fact are peevish. One man wrote, "don't ever forget the letdown coming." He may have intended it as counsel; to me it rang like a curse. Justly or not, in some ways I've been tempted to measure people's responses as thumbnail indicators of what they were actually "made of."

Of course, it's never that simple. It is the women I'm most leery of wounding, the women whose unseen responses crack my heart. However gently I may couch the news, however tentatively I phrase it, unless they are themselves happily situated, it is impossible not to worry about their emotional struggle. I've been there. I've been them.

What I'm describing here seems kin to the strange invidiousness of people's reactions to success of any kind. (I remember the director of a famous artistic retreat drawling caustically, as I ran into the copying room waving a newly published article: "You're having quite a year, aren't you?") And I do not exempt myself from this subtle, poisonous, often seemingly involuntary withdrawal. I've felt ugly jealousy at others' honors or achievements—people I like and whose work I admire—and it didn't have to do with whether I felt their glory was *merited* or not. It had to do with navel-gazing, with the sudden flash-inventory called up by another's success—inventory of my own days and works and whatever I hope—or fear—these might add up to. People hear about the triumph of another, and are knocked into a kind of delirious, and cruel, self-scourging. A roster of private dreams and wishes scrolls before them; their own lives come up wanting. When they react in sad or disturbing ways, people are no longer seeing or hearing the messenger: they are thinking out loud.

One wants to preserve the ethic of abject honesty. It's what women do best, and take great solace by. On the other hand, I now understand the importance of putting aside the initial maudlin seizure and at least *pretending* one is glad for a friend. Let function follow form, for the true pleasure will come later, when we have managed to climb out of our own navels, and to think a little larger. People in love long to be cheered on—not to be chastened, by guilt or anything else, into playing it down or renouncing it.

But I wind up doing just that. In efforts to make it sound not as damned wonderful as it is, I backpedal and equivocate. I say, *well, it's early yet,* and *it's very scary, of course,* and *a little at a time,* and *I have these fears,* and *who ever knows?*

What I want to shout is: Dear friend! *This is not like winning a lottery.* No bankable weekly checks arriving like clockwork! *Everything is contingent* in this new land, everything is provisional: it's a daily call, and nothing, absolutely *nothing's* guaranteed—or ever will be, even for people who've been at it a lifetime. It occurs to me now that even if one marries the beloved every day, all two individuals can ever have as proof and actuality—as living text, hard evidence of all their faith—is simply each single day together.

I also want to say: Dear friend, I can only steer my own little boat here—as I always have, as each of us is bound to. Let me have this moment; *bless* this passage for me now, won't you please? And I will try to find it in me, when time comes, to bless yours.

Or pretend to, until our better selves seep through.

A Time to
Every Purpose

A FEW YEARS AGO I wrote that I hated clothes-shopping worse than the taste of Milk of Magnesia, and that I wished we all wore togas. I swore I forged out to shop only for *extremely* special events, like a hot date, or a big trip, or falling in love. Last summer I went on a date, fell in love, and now plan a big trip. I've lost weight from sheer anxiety.

What happened was this: I quickly learned that the man in question tended to like women with a certain look. A kind of conventionally glamorous look. That is to say, hose, heels, clingy things—the full catastrophe, you might call it if you were a feminist who treasures her old flannel shirts beyond reason. (If you were a fairly typical hetero man you might call it "healthy, red-blooded" hetero maleness. Why women are never called red-blooded, I've yet to understand.) The trauma began when my dear new mate casually let slip the remark that the current state of my underwear was perhaps only fit for setting fire to. The second blow came the day I found myself staring without recognition at the woman in the mirror who was dazzling in a white silk shift and matching jacket. She could have been coasting on royalties from dozens of obscenely successful novels, holding forth cunningly in Parisian salons. I stood flabbergasted, unable to assimilate: your basic Pygmalion shock.

My boyfriend loved the clothes. We bought them together, splitting the considerable expense down the middle, during which I felt faint and feverish even at half price. And walking down the street with this new finery, we talked about the 360-degree, Incredible-Hulk-torque it applies to my brain to see myself, or rather, *believe* myself, in such stunning getups. I simply had never allowed myself to think of looking that way, let alone to spend money on myself that way. There were always a million more important expenses; never had I dared dream I could, or should, look so—glossy. Patiently, my boyfriend explained that growing up poor made it hard for people who were well into adulthood (and in every other way competent at it) to believe themselves worthy of nice things. I was a prime example of this sorrowful axiom, he could see, and he could also see it was going to take a massive mental overhaul to enable me to think and act differently. "Like dating East Germany," he murmured.

After he had apologized, and I had stopped threatening to extract his teeth without anesthesia, I reflected that though his comment had stung me deeply, and though it seemed to go against all my earlier declamations, he was indeed onto something. Looking better genuinely made me feel better, and the ripples flow from that concentrically, far and wide. I am at terrible risk confessing it here, I know, but I have had to eat some of my own dogma (Thou shalt not try too hard to look too good), and so far I have not gone crazy or been struck down by the gods of severe-correctness. I am still surprised, though, by the woman in white silk in the mirror, and there is still a dark breach into which my self-image falls and paddles around in confusion, between the previous self-perception and the improved one. Who is who? And do I really have to scrap my flannel shirts?

Women know that it takes constant work to look good, or at least, to look a certain kind of good. By this I do not mean the startling, mannequin-perfection of the saleswomen haunting upper-crust department stores, whose faces alone, with their black-outlined lips, look embalmed. But merely to be healthy and clean is no longer sufficient either, as our mothers or the Girl Scout manual may once have assured us. You start with healthy and clean, and you build on that—beginning, I suppose, with underwear.

I am inventing the formula as I go: On days it doesn't matter, jeans and a soft shirt and kick-around shoes. On days it matters, the new blouse, the blazer, the cocktail dress, the hot little sweater and skirt. You start throwing out or giving away—slowly, slowly—all those limp threadbare shirts with the little hole in the elbow; the flats worn through to the metal at the heel that you've held onto forever. (*Why* is it so hard to let them go? What portion of life do these sad rags represent, that you are so afraid to leave? Innocence? Poverty?) Meantime you keep depositing new items into your brave little collection, like coins in a piggybank—all the while, steadying your psyche with sleep, nourishing food, exercise. The cumulative result, as all this percolates together, is a slow transformation in the mirror.

"I believe in transformations," declared my dear friend Deborah as she plopped herself on my couch for a fashion show. How generous she was: oohing and aahing at the new outfits, pondering what would compliment them, praising my figure, my workout, my food habits. And yet this is the woman with whom I have talked, for hours at a time, about the terrible difficulty of making a gracious stand as we age in a world obsessed with appearances. Finally I implored her: was it a betrayal of character, or of women, to spruce up in these ways?

"Pish posh," she snapped—an expression I love. I think she means, do what works. Nobody argues with Naomi Wolf, author of *The Beauty Myth*, when she insists first thing in her writings and lectures that women must be free to make themselves as beautiful and comfortable as they possibly can, and to suit their own tastes to a tee. Where it gets tricky in the feminine debate is accepting the complex motives for taking on various images—and what in turn those motives may represent. Like sexuality, these are dark and fast waters, not easily navigated, nor judged. Offhand, the hardest task for workaday women seems to be the balancing of relentless cultural mandates—the pouty *poseurs* on MTV and billboards for cognac—against one's own way of life, one's own dreams. I would add that when you fall in love, priorities reshuffle like a week's worth of canceled airline flights, and all bets are off. Watch those little announcement-boards whirl!

To everything, I also see, there is a season. For now the flannel shirts stay, but they are stacked behind the silk ensemble, the black pants suit, and the short suede skirt.

Tired:
Very Tired

*H*AS IT happened to you? The alarm clock—pitiless plastic torture—shrills your exhausted mind back up just, it seems, as you'd eased it down. The hot, pounding shower, the icewater splashed into eyeballs, the atomic-strength coffee, the brilliant sunlight—none of them helps. You drag to work, eyes aching, brain blurring, fogged as a leaky pair of swim goggles. You bump into furniture, forget how to spell, choke on perfunctory chat. Everyone seems to be moving in a too-bright, viscous fluid, and you can't quite hear what is said to you. Even your heart seems to beat arrhythmically. Nothing matters, or makes sense. The only clear image you can conjure—like the only television channel in a totalitarian state—is that of returning to bed, the warm, soft, rumply nest. Alas! That nest is a good ten hours away now—wave it bye-bye—meantime the full day, and all its duties, await.

You're ruined again, stupefied by fatigue. The day is lost, and you must limit yourself to idiot chores, remember to breathe, avoid decisions bigger than whether to eat an apple or a banana, concentrate with your last ounce of will on steering safely home—where it's likely a whole *new* roster of duties awaits you, before you can finally unplug the phone, hit the bed you dreamed of all day—and pray for a better tomorrow.

It isn't only the occasional bad night that make days like these. None of us seems to get enough sleep anymore, at a time, not coincidentally, when we need it most. For Americans at least—and this is not something to be proud of—there is always too much to do; we're harnessed to our obligations as if to a team of hurtling comets. Result? We measure and hoard sleep, crave it more obsessively than Midas did gold. When the accursed alarm jolts my mate and me bolt upright on weekday mornings, blind and gasping (is there any device that can wake you *without* inspiring bitter longing to smash it into slo-mo karate smithereens?), the first thing we do together is *math.* "What time did we go down? Are you sure? What time is it now?" If we can persuade ourselves that we slept, say, six hours, we can pretend that our bodies will find it somewhere in themselves to stagger up and face the day. It's a pathetic attempt at psychosomatic hoodwinking, but any port in a storm. (Naps are very nice, but who has time? Sunday afternoon naps, I fear, have gone the way of the dodo bird.)

I will in fact wager that sleep is possibly the highest value for most of us these days. No fancy reasoning required: Supply and demand is the operant law. When I phone someone and realize I've actually *waked* them, the impulse is to wail and tear my hair, pledge a month's hard labor for the awful crime of interrupting precious sleep. For me anyway, the arms of Morpheus beckon as the ultimate reward. Let our younger pals brag about staying up all night listening to Spitmuffin, or chafing over the nature of truth. Their day will come—or rather, their night: the night they trade meaningful glances across a crowded room as the clock nudges 10:30, and they begin that discreet edging toward the door, murmuring apologetically that they have to work in the morning. Not that the workplace does not sympathize. Yawn on the job, and my guess is you're answered by sad smiles of recognition and a chorus of "Oh, yeah!" "Me, too!" "I hear that!"

We aerobicize. We volunteer. We birth, parent, vote, consume, eliminate, litigate, agitate, recreate. We're tired. Very tired. A friend points out that at our age, we've arrived at the rather bizarre fulcrum whereby we have already worked very hard for a long time, and can only look forward to working very hard for a long time. Not the cheeriest view of the continuum, I agree—if I think that way too long, panic sets in. But she's got a point.

Give me adequate rest, and life is the Hallelujah chorus—there is no limit to what I can do, or at least feel capable of: breaking a deadlocked jury, lubing the car, cooking a fabulous *cassoulet*, spritzing around town like Tinkerbell with a glad word for every butcher and baker and bum. Conversely, the universe sickens and sours—a too-bright, queasy, Antonioni film—when not enough shuteye's been had. The difficulty of the simplest acts baffles me: taking out garbage, getting the groceries through the front door. Worse, we wear our fatigue at this stage. When the kids have blue circles under their eyes, that's artful, smoky, sexy, maybe even slightly heroic. But when the not-so-young look tired, it's not a thing you care to gaze on very long—especially not in the mirror. A catcher's mitt, or the tread on tractor tires, come to mind. There used to be shortcuts to looking and feeling sprightly even when we were under-rested: a splash of eyedrops, the temporary caffeine buzz from coffee or cola. Now there are no shortcuts. The savings bank of good health, with its dividends of bright eyes, shining hair, clear skin, and a cogent mind, accepts only hard-currency deposits of regular exercise, solid nutrition, and eight full hours of old-fashioned, horizontal, REM sleep. A rueful friend calls this our "heavy maintenance" phase. I hate to think of the sequel.

Build in time-outs, advise the newspaper articles. Fine: Pack up and drive four hours to collapse in a bed-and-breakfast, where you can relax for a day—to gear up for the drive home, which deposits you exhausted. *Learn to say no,* the same human-interest writers scold. This proves trickier than it sounds. If you keep saying no to extracurricular gigs with friends, what's finally the point of having friends? And didn't squandering all his waking energy on work make Jack a dull boy?

Tired as we are, *dull* is something we may still fear most. Perhaps it's a holdover from the days of wearing paisley and dancing around in meadows to Jimi Hendrix. We still dread worse than polio the notion of becoming the adult homebodies we remember viewing as '50s kids: bland, torpid armchair dummies whose lifeless gazes were fixed on Lawrence Welk.

So we keep dancing. Turns out it's a marathon. Some of us are propped against each other, eyelids at halfmast; others resort to sleepwalking. Open my kitchen cupboard, and what stares back at you? *Many* jars of vitamins. A vitamin emporium. The labels read like an apothecary's dictionary. I take a handful each night that would choke Deep Throat. Whether these multicolored horse-pills actually help or not, I can't truthfully say. But it's part of the self-persuasion. Who cares if the effect is placebo? It's an effect!

He's Moving In

I STAND IN HIS KITCHEN as we box up the first few things—some spices, his cookbooks, a blender, pillows, bookends, a vase. Do you play Scrabble? he is asking, surveying his dusty cupboards.

Suddenly I feel like I'm leaning over the edge of the world's tallest building. The backs of my legs go weak and trembly.

This is the man I have said I would do anything for. The one I have said I would marry tonight, should we decide that. Yet I am terrified. Every neurosis rushes to the fore.

We are about to combine households. Every night we'll face each other, each day plan and negotiate as partners. We'll shop together, travel, share meals, bathrooms, holidays, illnesses. Our friends will start to recombine. I look at the things in the boxes. My breath runs shallow. I try with all my might to ward off the morbid flash, but it pops in my face with blinding clarity: Will the day arrive when we stand around dividing up these vases and cups and Scrabble games?

I remember too keenly a day some years ago, when another

man and I stood around putting things in two piles. (Everyone's done it, I know, but that doesn't make it less vivid.) I had thought that that man would be my lifetime partner. He wasn't ready, as it turned out. Getting over it, I recall, was like freefall at top speed with no parachute. The man and I are now dear friends, but for some reason that does not soften the searing image of the day we sorted through belongings in the—yes—little seaside cottage we were about to stop sharing. That day stands apart, even from many years' distance. I remember the *quality of the light,* so deeply burnt is it in memory, the sun beaming down heedlessly, the water glittering. The poor man felt wretched, but his need to leave was not then something he could alter, and we stared at one another in helpless dismay.

Lord, how frightened I am of repeating that day. But as humans tell each other repeatedly, in loftiest and simplest language, from Fred Rogers to Elisabeth Kübler-Ross, life is risk, and if you cannot undertake it—not just bravely, but with zest and joy and even mischief—why bother? And imagine this: you might actually be a little smarter, now that you're older. Not *wise,* exactly, but neither quite the gooey-eyed idiot of a dozen or so years ago.

Still, let's not gloss over the grit. When I began living alone after that sad parting those years ago, I was mortified. The prospect seemed so foreign, so cold, such an indictment. Very gradually I came to understand and accept it; finally, to relish it. Now as I recommence living as a couple, I am, temporarily at least, mortified. It seems intrusive; in many ways, it looks like harder work. All those chestnut terms that sound like a Girl Scout pledge—faith, courage, honor—I'll need those now, in the biggest way; need to locate them and take firm hold.

As I gaze at my sweetheart's boxes, I wonder about loss of privacy. Will I be able to think as cogently, as deeply, as *dreamily* when I've far less time alone? Can I keep my autonomy, the same centrality of self? Will I like too much the habit of thinking and speaking as *we*? Better than anyone else, alas, I know how I tend to rush to mend the breach, to please, to smooth things, make them kind and peaceable. I do not want to look down one day and notice my arms and legs going transparent. Been there, did that. Even among the feistiest, most formidable, the *rudest* of us, women in love play a see-saw game with the ever-looming threat of their own effacement.

Nagging paranoias I thought I'd already put to rest, bounce back up like ghostly ducks in a gallery. Do I always have to look pretty? Can I never again wear my beat-to-hell pajamas and crumbling sweats? I answer myself fiercely: If he had wanted to live with someone who goes around in an old U of Wisconsin sweatshirt, baggy flannel leggings, chartreuse socks and stretched-out penny loafers, well then, he would have arranged for that, wouldn't he. That was *not* how I represented myself while we were dating, and it would not be truth in advertising to lapse into it now. But good heavens, man, he can't always expect me to try to look like Gabrielle Anwar. I've not the bank account!

Still, the terrors rattle on: Do I have to learn to cook as well as he can? To play chess? Do I have to think in terms of "have to"? Will desire survive dailiness? Can I still find opportunities to see my sister? Will his little son like my little nephews? Will he be as proud of my books as I am of his plays? And not least: If we cannot just yet utter vows that were contrived during days when people seldom lived past forty—can we nevertheless feel it reasonable to look forward to a certain refuge, a respect and tender decency, a long and, in the main, happy life?

I suppose friends would say: welcome to couplehood.

Yes, I tell him slowly. I am no champion at it, but I can play Scrabble.

Conari Press, established in 1987, publishes books for women on topics ranging from sexuality and women's history to spirituality and personal growth.

Our main goal is to publish quality books that will make a difference in people's lives—both how we feel about ourselves and how we relate to one another.

Our readers are our most important resource, and we value your input, suggestions, and ideas. After all, we are publishing books for you.

For a catalog of our books, please contact us at:

Conari Press
1144 65th Street, Suite B
Emeryville, CA 94608
800-685-9595